DEMOCRATIC REPUBLIC OF CONGO RDC

KINSHASA, THE CAPITAL CITY OF THE CONGO RDC,

PRIOR TO THE CIVIL WAR

TABLE OF CONTENTS

A Mysterious Boy called Timo Mikwaya

Well known as – *KAMINA*

CHAPTER I

PROPOSAL ISSUES DUE TO DIFFERENT BACKGROUNDS

Denoza was a beautiful young lady. She weighed about one hundred twenty pounds, and she was about five feet four inches tall. Denoza's mother was a princess from an ancient Kingdom in Central Africa (Congo). Her father was a well known Chief in her Village. Denoza came from a very reputable, and well to do family. Mikwaya on the other hand was handsome lad. He weighed about one hundred seventy pounds, and was six feet and two inches tall. He came from a modest religious family. Although his family did not have much wealth, Mikwaya was known to be the well educated gentleman in his village. He had acquired his education in a very good school at the nearby Mission. Most of his instructors were western Missionaries who liked him very much.

All of them spoke highly bout his intelligence and his ability to master situations around him. He graduated with honors, and at the graduation ceremony, he was selected to deliver his class speech which had touched everyone's heart. Due to his achievement, Mikwaya had a promising future. He was offered a teaching position for the upcoming academic year. Prior to marrying the woman of his dreams, the daughter of the Chief of his native village, and being subsequently blessed with a gifted child, Timoli Mikwaya experienced a series of deceits and frustrations when he was attempting to establish a communication with Denoza, the chief's daughter in order to propose to her.

In fact, those depressing experiences were due to their two different social backgrounds. In order to establish some communication with Denoza, Mikwaya spent months to see how he could have possibly proceeded under such circumstance. The difference between their social statuses was a huge barrier, because Denoza had a royal blood. She had a very high self-esteem due to her social rank.

She could have never dreamt to marry Mikwaya regardless of his beautiful appearance, as well as his school achievement.

All this was not regarded as suitable qualifications that could permit such a serious association.

NIANGA DENOZA'S GIRL FRIEND AND A LIAISON AGENT

Mikwaya was using Denoza's girl-friend, called Nianga as an intermediary in the attempt to establish a communication with Denoza. He had assured Denoza's friend that he would do whatever he could in his power to marry Denoza, regardless of their social status. On one occasion, Mikwaya told Nianga that his fondest dream was to have three beautiful children with Denoza. Mikwaya told Nianga also that he was aware of all the barriers that he would have to encounter in trying to establish a relationship with Denoza. However, he said that he was determined to surmount them all regardless. Nianga was reluctant at first to convey Mikwaya's messages to her girl-friend Denoza, because she was aware of their different backgrounds and especially for the fact that Denoza had always maintained her high self esteem.

Timoli Mikwaya formed a habit of walking at least once a day up and down the main road facing Denoza, s huge property. He could have chosen a different road leading to the local church where he had offered to volunteer while on vacation. He had rather preferred to walk on the road where Denoza's house stood. Every time that Timoli came across Nianga, he was compelled to express his deepest feelings about Denoza, as much as he could in his own way. Although Denoza could never in her life time consider Mikwaya to be her future husband, she however formed the habit of listening to Nianga out of courtesy. As far as Denoza was concerned, any message originating from Timoli appeared to be a trivial nonsense.

Mikwaya continued walking on the main road always expecting to meet Nianga whenever he approached Denoza's property. Mikwaya felt heartbroken the day that he missed seeing Nianga. He would be very upset because Timoli knew that Nianga was his only hope to help him bridge his relationship with Denoza. However, whenever he came across Nianga, he would seize this opportunity to express himself.

Nianga noticed that Mikwaya had become a frequent passenger on the main road where Denoza's residence stood. One day, all of a sudden, she made a remark saying: "I can see Timoli that you really love Denoza," she joked. Timoli, you have become a frequent passenger in this road, she added.

Mikwaya smiled, and replied that of course that goes without saying Nianga; no one can actually hide a sincere feeling. In fact, I must admit it, and I really feel good walking down this road. He continued, Nianga you don't know how much I appreciate knowing you as the chief's daughter closest friend. Nianga, remember, Timoli said to her that you are so special to me, and you are my only hope. I have no other mean to connect with the Chief's daughter. She set herself way too high for a modest guy like me to reach her.

Timoli added that my stroll around here is of course self explanatory. He also said that it is in the attempt to catch a glimpse of Denoza, even though she would not budge to look in my direction. Then, he murmured, "I am sure in Denoza's eyes I just appear as though I am a piece of dirt, he mumbled." Nianga felt awkward to hear this remark, but could not comment. She chose just to smile a little.

One day, on a Tuesday, when Mikwaya saw Nianga at 4:30 p.m., it was about half a mile away from Denoza's home, and she was rushing to meet Denoza at her home. Timoli was delighted to see Nianga on the road again.

As soon as he had approached her in the attempt to carry on a conversation in a usual manner, Nianga however, exclaimed! I am sorry, Mikwaya, today is not a great day. I am in a hurry because I must meet Denoza at 5 p.m. I have an appointment with her. I must braid her hair, because afterwards there will be a ceremony in her home. The Chief of the Mountain Village will be the guest of her parents this evening. She has to get ready, and I must depart prior to that time.

Timoli looked at Nianga, and said I really marvel you. You are indeed privileged to be a Chief's daughter's best friend. I understand that those people from such a high rank always select friends among themselves. It appeared that you too must be from a wealthy family for Denoza to select you as her closest friend. I was told that the criteria to be friends of the Chief's family depend on how much wealth someone must have in terms of livestock or cattle and so on.

I was told also that the common questions asked I believe are: "How many cows, how many sheep, how many goats, how many pisciculture ponds, and how many farms that individual's family should own in order to be accepted in their association," am I right Nianga, Mikwaya asked? Well, I can't say, "No" to that remark, replied Nianga. Mikwaya continued Nianga, if I may ask, does your family own all of this wealth as well? Timoli continued "I am sure they have to have in order for you to be accepted as Denoza's closest friend?"

Nianga said to Timoli that frankly, my family just owns a little bit of wealth which cannot be compared with the Chief's wealth as you know it. Everyone should really know that. Denoza is a Chief's daughter and her mother is a princess therefore they have it all. She just happens to be privileged of being born in such a wealthy family. Timoli, Nianga continued, I shouldn't really reveal this, but I think I may, because you seem to be a very understanding person. Concerning my family, I do not actually know in details about the livestock they might really have. I would think my family had told me vaguely that we only have ten sheep, seven goats, six pigs and six ducks.

We also have eleven chickens and two Cocks, she added. Timoli repeated after Nianga; you have eleven chickens and only two male chickens? Wow, those male chickens must work overtime to produce eggs from all of those eleven chickens, laughter! What a good sense of humor, the lady said.

Nianga continue, further, my family also owns one medium size farm, whereas Denoza's family has about three huge farms, and one huge palm trees (oil) plantation. Further, they also own one coffee plantation and one sugar cane plantation. I mean, Nianga said, they own a lot. Probably it is because they also have workers for their upkeep, she added. Mikwaya said at least you have more than what my folks have. You actually should not consider yourself to be classified as poor. Timoli thought that this was probably the reason why Denoza's parents are permitting Nianga to be her closest friend.

Nianga explained to Mikwaya that I believe it is because we have been going to the same school since we were in the fourth grade. Currently, we are attending a Sewing School at the Sowa Mission.

We are now learning how to cut and sew women's camisoles and children's clothing. Denoza has three sewing machines which can make different stitches.

I, unfortunately do not own any. She is letting me use one of her sewing machines. Concerning our sewing ability, I am very good in creating different styles and she is very capable in assembling pieces. Denoza is also very patient in correcting any sewing defect. She is actually meticulous or perfectionist, so, to speak. Apparently, we make a good team together, Nianga shrugged.

Her father, Chief Mundu is fond of our school progress; probably this is also the reason why they overlooked at my social standard. Timoli, pleaded, Nianga could you relay a message to Denoza from me, please? Can you tell her that I really would love to speak with her personally? I know, Timoli noted, perhaps, Denoza's first question would be "how many cows does my family have or how many farms do my parents own, and how much of this or that and other things do I have. I am under the impression, said Timoli that, this is how she actually would disqualify me to be her spouse, if my answers are not satisfactory to her.

"Nianga knew deep down that this is exactly how Denoza would react, but chose not to comment. Mikwaya however asked Nianga whether or not she had any comments about the point he had just made?

Nianga said that she had no comments however, promised to relate his message to Denoza somehow. When Nianga told Denoza about Timoli's intention to marry her, she exclaimed, "Waya!" (Hail!) No way! Is that a joke, Nianga? Timoli Mikwaya, intends to marry who? Me? What does Timoli's family own? Do they have any cattle? I have never heard any one speaking of their wealth. Did you Nianga? Nianga replied diplomatically, they might actually have it, but you would never know.

In reality, some families choose to grow their cattle in different villages. Suppose that they do, how many cows do you think his family may have, Denoza asked? How many farms, or any pisciculture ponds they may actually own? Do they have pigs or goats, ducks and pigeons? My father is a Chief, Nianga as you know it well, and we also have servants as you notice. Nianga, I wonder how in the world this guy could conceive the idea of proposing to me? Does he mean that he would like to become one of my father's servants? It appears as though he does not know anything regarding the royal system. Everyone should really know that they do not just cross from a modest family to a royal family just like that. There is actually a very big gap in between, which can never be bridged in one second.

Does this man really mean what he says, or he just has a good sense of humor? Besides, Nianga we have some restrictions in dealing with the outsiders, she emphasized.

Denoza was somewhat disturbed to hear this. Then she continued, if they do not have any wealth, this means that they cannot have any servants. Nianga, am I right? Denoza looked straight in Nianga's eyes, and said," you should have just told the man right there and then that it would be just impossible for the Chief's daughter to marry a man from a modest family, period. At this point Nianga became fearful. She started to blame herself for daring to relay Timoli's message. She started to wonder whether or not her friendship with the Chief's daughter would be over. Nianga, Denoza continued, do not feel badly. I am not actually yelling at you, but I just would like to find out from you who seem to know him, did he ever mention to you what types of wealth do his folks have?

Nianga replied softly that I have not discussed any such thing with him. However, all I noticed about him is the fact that he appeared to be very kind and very humble. He also appears to be very religious. I see him going to local church on a regular basis.

Denoza said to her girl-friend Nianga, in case you were not aware, my mother is a princess, my father is a Chief as you know. Based on our sacred culture, I am supposed to marry a son of another Chief; and never should I marry a man coming from a modest family or any other. I must maintain the dignity of the royal background. Further, I have been well educated concerning these issues, and Mama has always stressed in the fact that chief's children should not demean their families' standard of living. Furthermore, as a chief's daughter, my demeanor should stand out. Do you understand my point, Nianga? Please do not be emotional, but realistic, she insisted. Nianga replied softly, I definitely understand your point of view, Denoza. I am actually being educated in this subject as well.

Denoza ordered Nianga to advise Timoli that he should actually find himself another woman of his own background with whom he would feel more comfortable. This would prevent him hearing all these restrictions. Nianga felt awkward to relate such a negative answer to Mikwaya who was anxious to see her afterwards. The next day, once again Nianga met him around the usual time. Timoli was taking his usual stroll and Nianga was going to the chief's house to meet with Denoza for a sewing session.

Mikwaya asked Nianga, to find out whether or not she had any message from Denoza based on their latter discussion? Nianga tried to be very diplomatic about relating that negative message to him. She said, squeezing her left hand: "Denoza feels that another woman would be suitable to be your spouse." Hearing such a negative statement, Timoli was somewhat depressed. He just shrugged, and added, well, God will do what God wants to do. He has the power to part the ocean, as well as the power to bridge all the gaps.

Timoli continued, it is strange, Nianga I had a dream the other night which does not coincide with Denoza's response. Nianga pleaded for Mikwaya to tell her that strange dream which he had had regarding Denoza.

The dream was as follow, he replied, "In my dream, the lady stood up, and then brought a child, and had it seated on my laps; afterwards, she went to get a tape measure. I noticed that the little boy was very handsome. He had beautiful sharp eyes. The child appeared to be very special; and many people were talking about him. That woman appeared to be Denoza, and I heard Denoza calling that child "Kamina!" That was the end of that dream.

I just wonder what could be the meaning of such a peculiar dream, Mikwaya said it sadly."

Timoli continued, please Nianga do not make any mention to Denoza about this dream at the present time yet. I would appreciate it, if you would refrain telling her so that she does not get irritated. Nianga promised not to tell Denoza about this strange dream. She probably would be deeply upset with me if I should mention it to her, said Nianga, anxiously. It would be preferable to handle these sensitive things gradually.

However Nianga continued, who knows, Mikwaya, this sounds as though you and Denoza could wind up becoming husband and wife one day. Timoli answered, that would be just a blessing to me, Nianga. Please keep on holding that picture so that you shall become our best friend. It would be a delightful future for me if this dream becomes a reality, he said. By the way, he added, I have just received a teaching position in the "Far Away Town," and I would love to take Denoza as my beloved wife with me there. I really would prefer to marry a native born of our village, especially the Chief's daughter, because she knows all about cultures, and she will be helping me to acquire the sacred knowledge, and also pass it on to our future children, Timoli concluded.

NIANGA REVEALED MIKWAYA'S SECRET TO DENOZA

FOR THE FIRST TIME

A week later, Nianga told Denoza that Timoli will be departing to "Far Away Town" in order to begin his teaching career. He told me that he would love to carry you to the Town as his beloved wife. Denoza exclaimed! Nianga you should have told him right then and there that I said he should keep his eyes off me; and find himself another woman of his background, she insisted! She sounded annoyed to hear this thing once more.

In effect, I would never want to embarrass my folks, said Denoza. If I mention this man's name to my parents, their first question would be who is he that man called Timoli? What does Timoli's family own? Nianga, you know what I mean, don't you? Denoza insisted?

I will never cover up anything regarding his family, if it does not own any wealth. She continued, Nianga, I would definitely reply to Papa and Mama that this man's family owns "ZERO wealth," to make a long story short. Do you think that this guy knows anything about chiefs' culture, Nianga? It appears as though he does not; otherwise, he would not have dared to propose to me, laughter! Denoza continued, and then of course, my parents would just dismiss him in a second. I wish this man would really stop these kinds of nonsense with a chief's daughter! Denoza said, Nianga would you please remind him to stop his drivel? I do not actually find this funny, she concluded frowning.

Nianga felt badly to hear the manner in which Denoza was undermining Mikwaya. She pitied him inside of her. Nianga replied, Denoza, I quite understand where you are coming from. However, I believe that your family may consent if you introduce Mikwaya as a Scholar, and a well educated gentleman in our entire village. In addition, he has been offered a teaching position in the "Far Away Town." Nianga told Denoza, "Think well before you actually turn this man, Mikwaya down just because of his family's background. He is going to take you in the Town not in the village.

You will meet a variety of people, and you will become a well known teacher's spouse." So think it over, Denoza.

Hearing these things, Denoza, started to realize that Nianga was making good sense, and a new perspective began dawning. Denoza started to see things differently in her mind. Then suddenly, she said to Nianga, well suppose I marry this man, and he takes me to the "Far Away Town", Nianga, I do not see him being able to provide me with servants who could be performing the house chores. Further, Denoza reminded her friend that as you can witness, in my parents' home, servants are in charge of doing house chores. Nianga, do you see where the dilemma stands at? She concluded.

Nianga replied, do not forget Denoza, Mikwaya will be a teacher, and he will have money. I believe he could also hire some domestics to help you out especially he is aware of your high rank standard of living in this village. He might want to give you a high class life as well in order for you to keep the same high standard, said Nianga. Did Timoli really feel that way or you are just assuming, Denoza asked? Do you think he really loves me and that he would really like to marry me?

Denoza asked Nianga in order to get a confirmation, and Nianga encouraged Denoza, replying, "of course he does", and that is exactly what you should tell your folks, but hurry, because he will be leaving the village in two months. It would be preferable that you do it as soon as possible, so that you do not miss the opportunity. I plead it with you. Apparently, she added, he perceived no other woman in his mind, but you. In fact, every words he said, does not sound prankish at all. He actually is mature enough to recall the barriers that stand between both families' statuses.

NIANGA ACTED AS AN ADVOCATE TO ARRANGE MEETING

Denoza asked Nianga, what she should do at this point. Do you think that I should consult my folks prior to speaking with Timoli, or I should first speak with Timoli prior to consulting my family? Nianga replied with joy, well, Denoza, this is another "EQUATION" that needs to be solved here, laughter!

Probably you should consult your folks first, but remember you should verbalize, and focus on positive things about Mikwaya. Nianga continued, if I were you Denoza, I would insist on his intellectual achievements, and especially his new teaching position in the "Far Away Town." This is really impressive. If I were you, Nianga continued, I definitely would not make any mention of his family's possession.

Denoza said to Nianga, obviously they will inquire about his family's social status; as you know the routine questions regarding this topic are inevitable. That would actually be another issue to deal with. My folks evidently, would inquire about the type of cattle, farms or any plantations his family may own. Advise me, Nianga, what do you estimate the suitable answer to be, in regard to this case? Nianga replied, "Everyone actually knows that Chief Mundu can identify exactly who has what in this village. You just remain focused on the issue of Timoli's new position in "Far Away Town." She continued, Denoza, just try to be precise and avoid elaborating any question pertaining to his family's status.

Apparently, Denoza followed Nianga's advice. She decided to speak secretly with her mother first. Her mother's first reaction was, "oh, no, no, Denoza," remember you have a royal blood! You must associate with the Chiefs' children, she exclaimed! I do not think your father would like to hear such a disgraceful thing. You are a daughter of a Chief, I, your mother am a Princess! Your demeanor should reflect a royal blood or the one for chief's family. You must remain in the circle. I am afraid this would be a disgrace to our family. PLEASE DO NOT DARE, CHILD!

Denoza grew upset, and said to her, "Mama, Timoli will not be living in the Village. Timoli Mikwaya will be a teacher in the "Far Away Town"; never will he live in the village again. If you understand this, Papa also will understand it, but if you start objecting my wish, Papa will also contradict it as well. It all depends in the manner in which you will actually present this case." Denoza said to her mother, delicately. Her mother told Denoza that prior to speaking to your father, I will have to pray to God, and ask him to tell me clearly whether or not it is permissible for a child having a royal blood to actually bridge a gap with an outsider.

If God gives me the courage to discuss this issue with your father, then I will do it; otherwise Denoza, we will have just to dismiss this issue once and for all, because it is going to irritate the entire family, and especially your uncle, Prince Mokwe. You know how he worships our ancestors' culture; "Royalty" is our motto. So we must maintain it. My brother Mokwe would find this issue disrespectful, my daughter. Denoza asked her mother, so mama when do you think God will give you the answer?

Do not worry about when. I know my God always gives me an instantaneous answer whenever I have a sincere desire to know something. I would ask you to wait until tomorrow morning, and I trust that my heart will have a suitable answer. If I do, I will then call to advise you regarding this matter, however, I beg you not to anticipate any answer.

The next day, Denoza met with Nianga, and reported to her all the details regarding her conversation with her mother, the Princess. She told Nianga that her mother was in state of shock, and was speechless. She said to me, "Denoza I, your mother, have been doing my job meticulously in transmitting orally to you, all the necessary details regarding our culture. There is nothing hidden that I have not actually revealed to you. Therefore, you should be capable to express and defend yourself anywhere without fear. Daughter, remember, the culture was formed way before I was born.

I did not create it. I just inherited it, the same way you are inheriting it from me. Please do not be ashamed to confess your roots; it is something that cannot be altered, her mother said. Denoza whatever you do in your life do not forget that you have a "Royal blood embedded in your veins." Nianga was listening with deep interest, then she asked Denoza, "Why did your mother wanted to remind you about all these things?" She is afraid that it might be a disgrace if I happen to depart from it. She also fears her brother, my uncle Chief Mokwe' reactions; the prince would probably go wild to hear that his niece is trying to bridge two opposite social backgrounds, which might lose the dignity of the royal background.

Nianga was sympathetic to both Timoli and Denoza especially to Timoli. She was however, learning the whole process. She had never thought it was such a big deal for Chiefs' children to marry somebody of different social background. She started to realize that Mikwaya was not quite aware of this procedure and their restrictions. Nianga knew that Mikwaya will be hurt to hear all these unkind words. This is a very touchy issue. And why in the world did Timoli have to take interest in this high class family? She herself started to get nervous, and began to wonder the reason why in the worl, she herself had gotten involved into this complicated situation. Nevertheless, Mikwaya expected criticism regarding his social background. Nianga felt that Timoli appears to be a courageous gentleman, and he has faith to overcome this dilemma. Apparently, Nianga was courageous as well; she continued encouraging her friend to remain calm and see what God will tell her friend's mother. Nianga said to herself, I hope Denoza's mother knows really how to pray in order to convince God! She decided to ask Denoza, "Does your mother really know how to pray? "Denoza answered that I do see her sometimes uttering few words; however, I do not really know the degree of her faith.

Two days later, Denoza's mother called her, and told her that I have actually decided to report this issue to your father. However, you must be ready to accept whatever decision your father makes. If your father replies, "Yes, I consent," all of us will shout, "Yes," but if he says, oh, no! Of course all of us will have to repeat the word your father has pronounced, "No, and oh, no way!" In addition her mother said, Denoza dear, I am just preparing you, because your father is an Imposing man. He is a Chief, his decision will prevail regardless. It is preferable for that man, Mikwaya to get himself ready in hearing either a negative or a positive answer regarding his proposal issue, her mother insisted.

The mother continued, besides, your uncle Chief Mokwe of the Zama Village he is another one that you should worry about.

You know how attached and stern he is to our family, and the degree in which he values our culture. In fact, all of us do to some degree. He is actually the one who might oppose to Mikwaya's marriage proposal; as you know he is never lenient in many things, and especially not when it comes to the respect of our Royal blood.

DENOZA 'S CONVERSATION WITH HER PARENTS

A day later, Chief Mundu called Denoza to inquire about this situation. He asked her, "Who is Timoli Mikwaya?" Denoza spoke highly about Timoli, focusing on his educational level and his bright upcoming teaching career. Chief Mundu listened carefully but told Denoza, your mother and I should have mentioned the intention of Chief Mokwe, your uncle, Chief Mokwe of Zama Village and his wife.

Ultimately, the family had always desired that you marry their son Miselo, your cousin. Denoza repeated, marry my cousin Miselo? Chief Mundu replied, "Yes", it is acceptable as far as our culture is concerned.

It is permissible for you to marry your uncle's son from your mother side (your cousin), but it is not allowed for you to marry your uncle's son from your father's side, because he is considered to be your real brother, and it is known as a taboo to do so. This is how our ancestors had established the culture which we must follow, and respect. This is how we actually honor their wisdom. What actually matters here is the fact that you both have a royal blood. This is really how the children of Chiefs should get married. It should be done among themselves in order to maintain the dignity or a high social standard. Denoza did not verbalize her comments, but she opposed the idea of marrying her cousin Miselo in her heart. She felt more affinity with Timoli than with Miselo anyway, as far as she was concerned.

Chief Mundu continued, besides, only the Chiefs' families are capable to afford a high quality dowry as you know the traditional wedding is divided into both, the bride's mother's side as well as her father's side, and the dowry is very costly, he explained. It is a very big commitment, you see my daughter for the groom and his family. The dowry is simply a means of scrutinizing a groom who is daring to marry a chief's daughter. In fact, even in the modest or poor families, the dowry must apply according to their means. The ceremony is always conducted under the presence of the Mbaku (judges), and usually it is done harmoniously. The Mbaku are very qualified individuals, who know how to evaluate situations, and make a fair decision to both parties. In addition, Mbaku are capable to arrange payment in installments when the groom's family is unable to meet his current obligations.

Chief Mundu was questioning about Timoli Mikwaya's family whom Denoza is about to get involved with. He wondered whether or not Mikwaya was really aware of Chief's system of dowry? Would his family be able to meet the dowry obligations? He continued, at least in this entire village I know who has what, but the Mikwaya's family does not own any cattle here, unless they have it elsewhere, Chief Mundu confirmed, shaking his head. This may cause us a problem, Chief Mundu said, holding his chin with his right hand, and shaking his head. Denoza was listening quietly to her father during the entire conversation.

Then suddenly, she replied "Papa", Timoli Mikwaya is that most educated gentleman in this Village. Almost everyone talk about him. He grew up in the missionaries' home at the Mission. He occasionally comes to the village during vacations. When he is vacationing, he is busy volunteering at the local church. He is the student who had delivered the speech at the last graduation ceremony which you had been invited to attend at the Mission, and the speech which you have been referring to.

Denoza continued you saw how highly his instructors spoke about him during and after the ceremony? In fact, he had received a Teaching position in a "Far Away Town." Furthermore, he would like to marry a woman of our village whom he can be proud of in the Town, she added. Timoli will not be living in the Village at all, but in the Town. Hearing this statement, Chief Mundu told her daughter, Denoza you go and think about what I had just told you regarding Miselo and dowry. Your mother and I will also think about it then we will subsequently decide.

Shortly after his conversation with his daughter, Chief Mundu heaved a sigh! He sensed that his daughter would not want to marry her cousin Miselo; she is favoring Timoli Mikwaya, instead. I can feel it. This is discouraging, indeed, he said.

Denoza and Nianga met a day later; and Denoza shared with her the discussion she and her father, Chief Mundu had regarding that issue. Nianga became aware of how much those who have a royal blood hold on into their heritage, reputation and image. She then realized how privileged she has been to be accepted as the Chief's daughter best friend. Denoza repeated what her mother warned her, "If your father says, 'Yes, all of us will repeat, yes, but if he should say, "Oh, no, we all will respond, oh, no way". This would mean of course that I cannot marry Timoli at all; and that would be the end of your liaison withTimoli, Denoza concluded. Well, in that case, Nianga said, I wouldn't know how to face Mikwaya and what to say? Denoza replied until I hear from my folks, we have another "Puzzle "to solve.

Nianga said, well just let us wait and see what the outcome will be, laughter! And both of them shrugged. When Denoza returned home that evening, her parents called to speak with her. During that family meeting, her father began saying, Denoza based on Timoli Mikwaya's upcoming bright teaching career, we have decided to meet Timoli Mikwaya first of all, and then we will meet his folks afterwards, because we need to find out few things from them prior to making any type of decision.

DENOZA'S FIRST MEETING WITH MIKWAYA

Denoza asked Nianga to arrange a meeting with Timoli Mikwaya. She continued, my parents decided to meet Timoli first, and then they will meet his family afterwards. Nianga got excited to hear that positive step. Denoza, she said, "It seems as though this is going to be good news," Nianga anticipated. She also added that, certainly Timoli's family would be very nervous to come and meet Chief Mundu and your mother for the first time. It is a normal feeling obviously, and anybody would actually react likewise. Well, I will try to help them overcome their nervousness, replied Denoza.

Nianga suddenly recalled something, and then confirmed, as a matter of fact, Denonza, I saw Timoli this morning.

I believe he was heading to the local church as he always does. Nianga continued, Denoza, I trust that if we should stand outside, at the dooryard of your home, or next to the main road, it would be very easy for me to approach him. That will actually create an opportunity to invite him on your property. Denoza felt uneasy with that statement, and then she asked, "Oh, do you want him to come on the property?"Nianga replied that we can let him step at the threshold of the gate, if you so desire. At first, I would whisper a few words to him, and then I would encourage him to enter in the property. Ultimately, you two will have an opportunity to meet and establish a private communication. At this point, my advocacy or a liaison role would be finally ended, laughter!

Half an hour later, Nianga perceived Timoli walking down the road towards his family's home. Nianga shouted, eh, Timoli! Timoli noticed that Denoza was standing outside with Nianga for the very first time. He waved, and then Nianga ran towards outside Denoza's property whereas Denoza was stationed facing the scene; and observing his reaction. As soon as Nianga approached Timoli, she anxiously, whispered, Timoli come on into the property, and let me introduce you to Denoza, she said.

Mikwaya could hardly believe his eyes and ears. He asked as to double check her statement, Nianga are you sure that I can come into the Chief's property? Nianga replied, for today it is O.K., she insisted, Timoli come on in. Although he had the courage to walk in, apparently he was shy, as he shook hands with both young ladies, simultaneously.

Nianga noticed that Timoli was nervous because his speech was not as fluent as usual. He could hardly pronounced either names, instead of saying, hello Nianga, he incorrectly said, hello,"Me-m– Mianga!" Then when he was introduced to Denoza, the poor guy appeared as though he was losing his head, perspiration started dripping along his sideburns. Too good to be true, and he could hardly get it together, instead of saying hello D e n o z a, Timoli nervously mispronounced Denoza's name as he shook her hand, he said. "Hello, B-B-Bemosa!"

Poor guy, Nianga who knew his secret, observed that Timoli was so frantic in front of the woman of his dream. Denoza noticed that Timoli was as tall as her father, Chief Mundu, in fact as most of the people on her mother's as well as her father's family.

After introducing them to each other, Nianga noticed that none of them had the courage to start a conversation. They did nothing but smile at each other. After a few minutes, Timoli gathered his manhood's efforts and said to Denoza, you have such a wonderful girl-friend. Denoza confirmed that "Nianga and I have been friends since our childhood." Timoli softly told Denoza that probably Nianga had told you that I have received a teaching position to "Far Away Town." I do not want to go alone. I must travel along with my wife. Denoza knew where he was coming from then smiled. Shortly after, she asked Mikwaya, who is your wife? Timoli replied eagerly that my future wife is the one that God will be offering me shortly, in a few days, I believe. Who knows he continued, and then, smiling it could be "Denoza," Chief Mundu's daughter, if only Chief Mundu would accept to break the barriers, and allow me to become his son-in-law.

Denoza and Nianga stared at each other, and then laughed! Denoza took advantage to anticipate the meeting with her family. Denoza knowing her father well, decided to prepare Mikwaya prior to meeting her family. She told him, "My parents have a tendency of asking a lot of questions.

Therefore, you should be prepared, and have something to address to my father. If I were you, she said to him, the first thing to remember is "you are a scholar in this village, and everyone knows who you are." Before she had a chance to comment, Denoza decided to invite him in; she said, **"Timoli** you may actually come in the house, my parents are present, you may actually meet them today, if so desire. Timoli could not believe his ears, and anxiously and nervously, he asked Denoza, "Do you mean that I can actually meet your parents today, Denoza?"

Apparently, Timoli was not prepared for such a surprise. He did not expect to meet her parents that soon, and therefore, he pleaded, Denoza, "Could you possibly postpone the invitation until tomorrow? I would like to look decent to meet the Chief and his wife.

Nianga was excited as she was observing Timoli's reaction. It was too good to be true after nearly three months of resistance. That day was the first time since Timoli had been walking down the main road to actually appear happier than ever regarding this situation. His joy exceeded his expectations. It was actually too good to be true. Timoli knew that God was on his side.

God had answered his prayers. His faith in God had strengthened from this experience.

As he rushed to bring such great news to his own family, Mikwaya was overwhelmed with joy. He could not wait to get home and announce the good news. He felt very confident because things were turning to the bright side. He also said to himself, God indeed has the power to alter every situation, even to allow Denoza, the chief's daughter to dare to marry a modest guy. It appears as though God is bridging the gap between our two different social classes. This indeed will make a history, "*Timoli Mikwaya has just married Denoza, the Chief's daughter*!" He started to picture the whole image. He was delighted to notice the way things were working out.

CHAPTER II

MIKWAYA'S FAMILY REACTION

Timoli was imagining how his family would praise him for having such courage to propose to a Chief's daughter. However, the whole situation turned out to be a disaster, and depressing news to his entire family; That were his parents, brothers, sisters and especially to his first cousin Lipopo.

When he had arrived home, he noticed that his father was standing near the window, whereas the rest of his family members were seated. His mother was making dough to make Mikate (traditional donuts) for the next day. His two brothers and his sister Kizeka were busy listening to their cousin Lipopo, a soccer player, whose team had just won the soccer game that day, and he appeared overwhelmed with joy.

As soon as Mikwaya arrived, prior to announcing the breaking news, he neared his father by the window, and saluted him happily. He then faced those who were seating; suddenly he shouted, "Where is Mama?"

His mother answered in the kitchen, "I am here in the kitchen making mikate dough, my darling." When he had finally received everybody's attention, he then questioned them, "Are you ready to listen to the good news?" Everyone replied, yes, we are. What is it all about? His cousin Lipopo asked him. He continued, are you implying my soccer team's victory? Right, Lipopo asked. Before Timoli got a chance to share his joy in relating his personal and exciting story, his brother Masala, eagerly began telling him about what happened at the soccer game. Masala was known as a fanatic of soccer game.

His cousin Lipopo was a well known soccer star in the entire area. Therefore, Masala was his cousin Lipopo's fan as well. Timoli's brother Masala was so excited in describing in details, how the soccer game went that day. Masala knew that Timoli could not attend the soccer game competition between Chief Mundu's village soccer team players and Chief Mokwe's village soccer team Players. Masala went on praising their cousin Lipopo, the well known soccer star in their village.

Masala described with emotionalism how Lipopo has been scoring during the entire soccer game.

Furthermore, Masala continued, Timoli, my brother, you should have witnessed the determination in Lipopo's face to win that game! He really had the control of that ball. Masala wanted to portray the entire picture of the soccer game to his brother Timoli. And then, he began to illustrate all the details. Timoli, Lipopo kicked the ball in the opposite direction from his opponent, and he rolled it a little first, to the right, and then to the left and in the middle. All of a sudden, he bent awhile, and then swung a little from left to right. Finally, he jerked forward for a few minutes, and then he hit the ball with his favorite left leg.

Ultimately, before we knew it, Lipopo has scored in a few seconds! Masala was so excited, and wanted to really convey that feeling of his excitement to his brother Timoli so badly. I don't really know how to explain, said Masala. Words cannot do justice; the fans went wild cheering and chanting to express their joy, "Lipo-Lipo, Lipo, oh!" Masala went on describing all the details with emotionalism.

Timoli, Masala added, you should have watched me jumping up and down like an elementary school kid. At the end of the game, cousin Lipopo was lifted like a King! In fact, Referee of

Chief Mundu's village was here momentarily, and he had just left an hour ago. He came to congratulate Lipopo for his ability to score successively. He also reported that Chief Mundu was overwhelmed with joy, because the team of his village had won the game. He felt that the team actually had honored him and his constituents.

Moreover, Referee reported also that Chief Mundu will offer the team a goat with palm wine on Sunday, in the honor of the team and especially for Lipopo, the soccer game star. Chief Mundu promised also to pour his blessing on each one of them by applying Lupemba (a touch of ash on the right hand of each soccer game player) designed specially to thank God and the ancestors for giving the team the strength, the ability, and the wisdom to swing the ball meticulously which had eventually helped the team to win the soccer game. The Lupemba (blessed ash) will help to bring them further blessings as well as Victory in the future according to the culture belief.

Timoli replied that I am already aware of all these details. I overheard it while I was coming from the church. However, that is not the news I intend to share with you currently, he said to them. It is actually something regarding my personal life.

Something awesome has just occurred. His father faced him attentively; and asked him what is it? So tell us the news, said his father. You appeared happier than usually. Timoli replied the reason is that I had always wanted to propose to Denoza, the Chief's daughter however, I really did not know how to go about it. Evidently, it has been quite sometimes since I have been praying to God for guidance and courage to face the challenge. As you know, I have been going to local church for rendering my service to God. I really notice that God actually has rewarded me. I am therefore convinced that God is granting me the desire of my heart, Timoli added eagerly.

What makes you think that way son, his father asked? Timoli's father got upset to hear this. He looked straight into his eyes, and said, "Oh", what seems to be wrong with you, Timoli?" How dare you proposing to the Chief's daughter? Do you have a slightest idea regarding the wedding dowry?

Timoli, his father continued, marriage proposal to a Chief's daughter must be between their own kinds. A modest man cannot imagine proposing to a Chief's daughter; that would seem as though you are going beyond your means, he father added furiously.

His mother came out of the Kitchen quickly, and said, "Timoli darling, marriage portion requires money, so much money indeed, plus livestock dowry and thousands of other items to follow, including "twenty six Cows." All of these things must be presented at the celebration of both traditional weddings. Usually, the celebration from the bride's mother's side comes first, subsequently comes that of her father's side. Then each side has their own requirements, based on how much they want to scrutinize the groom's commitment to their daughter. There is a dowry in each side which the groom's family has to honor. Timoli, you must think deeply prior to taking this approach, his mother whispered in his ears.

Then she continued it is very scary indeed, looking towards that direction. How in the world can we provide the twenty six cows? Do not look for any trouble, please son, said his mother. Our family cannot afford any cow or any other items which you must offer in order to marry the Chief's daughter. It is just complicated, and it is very costly I would say. Chiefs' families have cows everywhere, and we do not own any. Please my dear son, you are very intelligent, we know it, your instructors at the Mission know it as well, and so does everyone else.

Think deeply and you will eventually realize that the dream you are evoking here is not realistic. Besides, it is not guaranteed that the Chief will consent to your proposal. Please do not waste any more of your time looking towards that direction.

In addition, his mother insisted that Chiefs' children have to marry among themselves because they all can afford to exchange wealth. Further, during the traditional wedding ceremony Chiefs and their families dressed up majestically. Timoli, why would you even want to embarrass your family? You know quite well that we are not in the same class status, said his mother, looking straight into his eyes. Timoli, these are things to consider when looking for a young lady to marry here in the village. His mother stressed this concern.

Timoli, even with your educational achievement, you just can't. You should understand this son, please, his father said. When it comes to their dowries, chiefs do not care about educational achievement. They want rather tangible items in exchange of their daughters' hands. There are plenty of young ladies who come from modest families just like ours. If you open your eyes wide open, I am quite sure you will meet a very pretty young lady to marry.

There is absolutely no Chief around our area who would ever want to belittle himself to such a degree. Chiefs do not dare having close association with modest families. Son, please you should just forget that idea of becoming a Chief's son in-law. Please purge that idea out of your mind completely, his brothers Pitelo and sister Kizeka, added to this. Kizeka continued, Timo, I am sure everyone around here and especially those in Zama Village would find it ludicrous if they find out that you are trying so hard to associate with the Chief's family.

Mikwaya was fuming inside of him to notice the manner in which his family viewed the Chiefs in general, as though they were actually God. They could never imagine that things may one day change in the society. As far as Timoli's family is concerned, things will always remain in the status quo regardless. Mikwaya had found it very difficult to persuade them in terms of viewing things differently. Nevertheless, in order to prevent confusion Timoli had opted to remain quiet most of the time.

There were all kinds of comments to discourage Timoli as well as preventing him in pursuing his dream.

His cousin Lipopo whispered constantly in his ears, do you have any idea about traditional wedding dowry that a groom's family must offer in order to marry those young ladies from a high rank? The celebration of the traditional wedding is indeed, a very serious matter Timoli, I tell you! The groom and his family must really feel the heat. They get really scrutinized, I tell you. The reason they scrutinize the groom and his family is to ensure that the marriage is indeed built on the rock, and that the chief's daughter will be protected by the husband no matter what happens in life. This is the only way a groom can prove his commitment. It is actually for a security reason; do you understand Timoli, asked Lipopo?

Concerning dowry, besides from offering a set amount of cash, livestock is a must. It is mandatory to offer a set number of Cows. The number of cows to offer varies from family to family according to what the "MBAKU" or judges have decided concerning that particular case. Usually they decide thirty, twenty six cows or something close to that effect. Half or fifteen go to the mother's side and half of the dowry goes to the bride's father side. As I had previously indicated, this is to ensure the authenticity of the marriage. Afterwards, come millions of other items to follow one item after another until the entire official list has been called.

The list will also include: twelve gallons of traditional Palm Wine I think, one Coleman lamp, fifteen pieces of Wax (a very high quality of African women's fabric) Etc.

Mikwaya's cousin, Lipopo seemed to know a lot more about the way traditional marriage is celebrated. Further, Lipopo continued they also request other items such as, two huge sacs of Salt and many different gadgets in order to satisfy the cultural requirements. Cousin Lipopo went on elaborating the situation, and stressing all the details.

He actually did this intentionally because he wanted to get Timoli to change his mind regarding Denoza; so that he could propose to any other modest young lady. Timoli, Lipopo continued, I tell you the requirements are just awesome! Timo, how in the world can you ever acquire all of these things? You have just graduated from school? Do you really think that shortly after you could be financially capable to meet of these enormous obligations? Timo, think once, think twice and please think thousand times prior to making this unwise decision.

You will be better off marrying the girl next door. Her parents are from the same background as we are. Her name is Mubile Amba. She was studying at the Mission as well unfortunately she dropped out, because her family could not afford the tuition. The tuition is just too high to some families who desire to send their children to the Mission in order to have a good education. I wish all those missionaries could have compassion to all our families. Mubile Amba you see, she comes from a modest family therefore the dowry would have to be moderate. Mbaku or judges know better, and they would never get into cows category.

Timoli's father said to him, we understand that you couldn't have learned this culture at the Mission. This cultural stuff you learn it neither in Town nor in School, at the Mission. This wisdom, sacred wisdom must be learned here in the Village. Mikwaya's father whispered in his ear, my son, you learn all the sacred culture from us, either from your mother and father, or from your uncle, your big brother or big sister. I don't care how much book knowledge you have acquired you must seek the knowledge of your culture. It will be your duty to pass this sacred knowledge along to the young generation to come, and I mean, your children or your nieces and nephews. As far as I am concerned, your instructors at the Mission know nothing about this sacred knowledge from our ancestors, because it is transmitted orally or by a word of mouth only. Do you understand me, son? The father insisted, shaking his head. When you will have children, make sure you transmit this sacred knowledge from our ancestors, to your kids, and do not forget to advise them to do the same for their own children, his father added.

Timoli's mother looked at Mikwaya's father eyes first, and then to her son. Finally she said, "I think your father and I should really reveal few things to you Timoli. It is regarding Denoza's background. She continued, calmly, Timoli, please listen carefully and learn. Denoza's mother is a princess; Chief Mokwe of Zama Village is a prince. They are all related, and both of them have a royal blood running in their veins. Your father and I have no royal blood running in our veins. Therefore, son, prior to proposing to a young lady in our area, you must be aware of all these things. Celebration of traditional wedding is a very big thing in our culture. However, if both groom and bride's families come from a modest background the dowry can be negotiable based on what the groom's family can afford at that particular time.

Installment payments of the wedding requirement can also be arranged even after marriage. Now you understand why all of us in this family are so shocked and disturbed to hear that you are proposing to the Chief's daughter? Timoli that level is extremely too high a modest family like ours for you to dare proposing to, concluded his mother. You cannot go around the village taking action without consulting us.

There are certain restrictions you must respect! His mother whispered. We understand you have acquired a lot of book knowledge at the Mission but we have the cultural knowledge. It is the Wisdom you need prior to proceeding in life.

MIKWAYA RECEIVED NEW CULTURAL EDUCATION FROM HIS SISTER

Mikwaya's sister Kizeka added, Timoli have you ever observed the celebration of the traditional wedding among the High class families? Timoli replied no, I have not. I actually missed few of them because every time one of the Chief's daughters was getting married, I was away at the Mission. Well, anyway, said Kizeka, the ceremony starts in the following manner: both groom and bride's families gathered together on a set date of celebration. Usually, the celebration is held on Saturday afternoon. At this time, the groom's family must be in readiness in terms of offering a chunk dowry to the bride's family. The offer includes livestock dowry and liquidity. On the other hand, the bride's family must also be in readiness in terms of the preparation of special dishes in order to honor that particular event; and receiving the in-laws to be.

The special dishes include the famous protein dishes which are well known such as: "NTERE" (pumpkin seed) the preparation of the meals for this big event is directed by special Cooks who can make different variety and flavor of NTERE Dishes. The most known varieties as you know it well are: NTERE and NKO (Pumpkin seed with Chicken) - *NTERE* and NTAB (Pumpkin seed with goat meat). - *NTERE* and MBISI (Pumpkin seed with baked fish - *NTERE* and MIKOSO (Pumpkin with shrimp or baby shrimp). - *NTERE* and BOW (Pumpkin seed with Mushroom – different kind of mushroom – Vegetarian style) - *NTERE* and *BISAKA* (Pumpkin seed with vegetable - usually spinach, (Vegetarian style).

Then come other meat and sea food varieties

Ngomb (beef, stew and baked) - Ntab (goat stew and baked - Ngul (pork stew and baked) - Nko na mwamba (Chicken in peanut butter sauce). They also cooked assorted vegetables namely: Pondu (cassava leaves), Epinard (Spinach), Biteko - teku (short kalaloo-steamed), Kalaloo na Mwamba (in peanut butter sauce), Nkofi na na mwamba (Collard Green in Peanut butter sauce)

Nkofi na Mwamba - ngasi (Collar green in palm nut sauce) then Dongo - Dongo na Mikoso (Okra in baby shrimp). The dishes are served with: Corn meal - Fufu, Millet, Cassave- Fufu, Corn-Cassava-Fufu, Rice, Plantine (mashed, fried, and boiled), Mbala (Sweet Potato), Bikwa (Yam) and Kwanga (baked cassava dish). Beverages are: Traditional Palm tree Wine, Coffee, Tea (Assorted herb-teas) and spring Water. Desserts are: Fruits: *Papaya, Mango, Banana, Orange, Tangerine, Pineapple, Sugar Cane, Mikate (sweet donuts).*

Based on our sacred culture, the groom's family must offer marriage portion (dowry) to the bride's family in order to prove his commitment. Good nuptial requires the offering of livestock dowry including a set amount of money decided by the traditional judges called "Mbaku, in addition to other things such as two Bipupu (Machetes) and Twenty Wax (African women's high quality Fabric) plus others gadgets mentioned on that official nuptial list.

Although the bride's family both sides, mothers and fathers organize the nuptial ceremony on two different dates, the Mbaku (Judges) must appear on each nuptial ceremony.

The same routine must be followed. At each wedding ceremony, the bride's family is obligated to offer s a big dinner to the groom's family and their guests. However, both families incur nuptial expenses. One family would offer dowry and the other family will prepared the wedding diner.

The announcer, usually a group of judges who conduct the traditional wedding ceremony, stands in the middle, then one of them, eventually the moderator will start calling from the official list of dowry, one item after the next. This is how the judges actually proceed: The very first thing they would say in order to attract everyone attention is: *"And now we will begin!"*

May the groom's family offer "The thirty COWS" – at this point, usually, the selected main cowboys will come in dragging one or two cows to represent the rest, and the audience will start applauding for acceptance ; other people on the other hand, will be applauding. Then the moderator will continue calling one item after the next until the completion of all the items requested.

And now, may the groom offer fifteen Waxes (pieces of African Women's high quality Fabric)? Then they will go on.

And now, may the groom's family offer Two Bipupu (Machetes) then One Coleman Lamp, they will continue to call all the items requested on the official list, and every time an item is called and shown, the audience will applaud and praise the groom's family how well to do they appear to be!

Finally Kizeka, his sister asked him, Timoli were you aware of all these details? Timoli replied not really. However, deep down he started to realize the magnitude of marriage proposal dowry especially in such a high level. Then, he replied to his sister, calmly that I participated on the traditional ceremony of my friend Ya Kizuini, his wife's family did not ask any cow, he concluded. His sister confirmed that the reason it was so because the groom came from a poor family whereas the bride came from a modest family. It was understood that his family could not have afforded any cow at all. Timoli's sister stressed the reason why she felt obligated to explain this matter to her brother. It was to educate him, as well as to broaden his knowledge regarding the culture on marriage proposal.

Mikwaya's sister knew the necessity of educating his brother. She concluded that with this knowledge, Timoli would know how to make his selection in the near future in regard to marriage proposal.

His sister continued, traditional wedding is a very big event, and it cannot be overlooked at. In fact, both the groom and the bride's families accumulate more expenses than the church marriage. On the day of celebration, you will notice all the Chiefs of the nearby villages and their families will be invited, and will be gathered at the ceremony.

All of them will be dressed up in LIPIAH Fabric (Chief's outfit). Few Chiefs are well known as traditional Judges, called Mbaku. They are divided in two opposite sides, one part represent the groom's side, and the other part represent the bride's side. Their job is to make sure that all the wedding requirements were reasonably asked, and that all of them have been met satisfactorily, prior to sealing the nuptial.

After the completion of the wedding dowry ceremony, the audience remains quiet, and the Judges must stand in the middle. One of the Judges or the moderator will start making the announcement in the following manner: "At this time the bride will introduce the groom to her family and to the audience gathered here." This is actually a very crucial moment; during this time, the groom will be seating in a secluded area, unknown to the bride. Then the bride will stand, and will start searching among the bachelors in order to find her fiancé, and then bring him to the view. At this time, the audience would remain absolutely quiet, and they will be observing how fast the bride would actually spot the groom, and bring him before the audience. It is usually a matter of five to ten minutes.

As soon as she discovered him, she will give him a very big hug, and both would hold hands while walking before the judges and the audience. This is a very exciting moment when the bride and the groom arrive before the judges; a moderator would raise the groom's hand shouting,"Now, here is the groom whom we all have been waiting for!" Then the audience and both family members would shout and applaud, and some people would be whistling to express their joy!

Subsequently, depending on which family side is celebrating the traditional wedding at that particular time, things will be done accordingly. If it is on the bride's mother side, the bride will perform the next step: A Judge would give a glass of wine to the bride, and she in turn will pass it over to her uncle, usually her mother's brother or her first cousin. The culture states that the uncle must sip some wine, and pour about one quarter of the content on the ground in order to honor his ancestors. This step must be performed prior to pronouncing the sacred statement "I, the bride's uncle on the mother side and all my family members consent this marriage, and it is now sealed."

If the celebration is on the father's side, the bride will perform the same steps, and the glass of wine must be given to her Father's brother or his first cousin in case there is no brother available at that time.

At the end of the dowry ceremony, the meal will be served. Further, at the end of the diner time, the Traditional musicians will begin playing traditional instruments such as Mpuita, Ngoma, Trumpet, Muzakisa, and Mfunga. The combination of these traditional musical instruments produces a marvelous, powerful sound, and the melody which travels miles away.

The minute the musicians start playing, all the chiefs and their wives would hit the dance floor. Shortly afterwards, all the elderly people will join. The favorite dance is called "MUBIRI" it is also known as "The ancestors' dance of honor." The elderly people usually just dance for a while then they would rest. The youth would continue with their current dance and style. The newlywed usually dances with the youth.

Then after a while, the Judge, usually the moderator would make a second announcement to interrupt the music and listen to the

Chief's speech. The bride's father or uncle would now seal the traditional wedding and pronounce the bride and groom legally bound as husband and wife. If the couple is religious, the church wedding will subsequently follow within a week or two.

On one hand, Timoli Mikwaya found all this detailed cultural education very informative. On the other hand, however, his new cultural awareness somewhat disturbed his view about proposing to a chief's daughter. It became very contradictory to his dream.

The statements he heard from the family members and especially from his cousin Lipopo, some of them were very negative; and did not sound supportive of his present dream. Timoli could not find any excuse to justify the reason why he had to marry a daughter of Chief Mundu, instead of another young lady of the same social background. He was puzzled, and remained quiet for a long while. Finally, he recalled that he was being expected at the Chief's home the next day. Therefore, he felt that he had to honor that invitation somehow. He wondered," how could he possibly convince his folks?

His family's advice and the new theory about the culture that was revealed to him, all these things seem to stand in his way. This dilemma was his first "EQUATION," that needed to be solved.

CHAPTER III

MIKWAYA'S FIRST MEETING WITH CHIEF MUNDU AND HIS WIFE KIBO

Timoli decided to go and meet Denoza's family regardless to his family reluctance.   He was well dressed and appeared professional, however, deep down he was nervous, and wondered what questions would he be asked? He said to himself; now that my family had made me aware of this special culture, how much chance do I have to overcome the obstacles? Humanly speaking he felt helpless.

Chief Mundu and his wife received Timoli the next evening. They asked him several questions about his desire to marry their daughter. Timoli assured Denoza's parents that he and his future wife will be living in the "Far Away Town." He felt that Denoza and he were chosen by God to become the parents of gifted children. The Chief reminded him about the regulations involved in marrying the Chief's daughter based on the culture. However, theChief and his wife told Mikwaya to bring his folks the next day so that they could meet them as well. Eventually, the encounter was to discuss the proposal matter in the details.

NEGATIVE REACTION FROM MIKWAYA'S FAMILY

When he arrived home, his family noticed that Timoli was happier than usually. They knew that he must have good news to share with them. He first spoke to his cousin Lipopo, saying, I must speak with Mama and Papa regarding the marriage issue which we had discussed yesterday. His cousin was excited to hear it. He told, Lipopo I met Denoza and his parents. His cousin replied, do you mean that you spoke with Chief Mundu, his wife and their daughter Denoza? Then what did they say? Lipopo asked. Well, Timoli replied, actually I was asked to bring Mama and Papa to meet with Denoza and her parents. Mikwaya said to Lipopo I wonder if they still could come after all their lectures of last time.

Lipopo had a negative attitude from the beginning. He answered, oh, Timoli you really don't know Chief Mundu. Chief Mundu from what I hear could get nasty sometimes. Your parents will be afraid to meet them because Chief Mundu will pepper them with questions which may be complicated for your parents to answer. I think you should not bother telling them, and I am sure they will react badly. Mikwaya was disturbed, did not know how to approach his parents with this issue again. He knew that things have gotten out of his hands. God is the only being who can solve this mystery.

Then he remembered one thing his Pastor had told him, "to find a correct answer when facing difficult issues and confusions, you must pray to God." He is the best Advisor and the best remedy you can ever have in your life. God knows exactly how to turn things around and upside down." So Mikwaya took the time to pray the best he knew how. He did this prior to inviting his parents to go with him; and meet Denoza's parents.

On one hand, Mikwaya realized and understood where his family where coming from. Obviously, they do not own even one tenth of the chief's wealth. They are afraid that the Chief's family may be disdainful. Also, they felt that if the people in the village would find out that the Chief did not consent Timoli marriage proposal to his daughter, due to Mikwaya's social class status, they would therefore mock at them. In addition, they would wonder the reason why Timoli's parents had let their son take this approach? On the other hand, Mikwaya sensed that his family might be over reacting, because they had not given the situation a chance for them to make that sort of judgment. Nevertheless, he said to himself, well, if it is God's will, nobody can ever prevent it. This statement was Mikwaya's consolation in the midst of all those confusions.

MIKWAYA'S DEVOTION TO GOD - HIS FAITH

Mikwaya learned how to pray since his childhood. His parents were religious. His devotion to his God grew deeper since he spent more time at the Mission. When he was on vacation in his village, Mikwaya never missed attending local church, and rendering service.

That is why when he found himself facing a serious problem which he couldn't handle humanly; he would find time to pray to God for guidance. Mikwaya had a lot of respect for his parents. He would never dare to say any word that would irritate his beloved mother or father.

When he was experiencing a resistance from his parents in regard to the marriage proposal, he decided to pray to God who alone could touch his parents' hearts, and illumine their minds.

He used to utter the following words on a regular basis, "Dear Lord, if Denoza is not the wife you have chosen for me, let Chief Mundu and his wife Kibo oppose to my proposal to their daughter." If Denoza's parents oppose, this would be an indication that I am not to continue looking at her direction. In that case, I therefore would have to follow my family's advice, and I would no longer think about Denoza in order to prevent demeaning my family. If, however Denoza's family's consent, this also will be an indication that my dream would be confirmed, and therefore I will have to precede my dream. Timoli was positive that the wealth issues and cultural barriers could never affect God's decision.

Further he prayed, "Dear Lord, you know how much I loved my parents, and I would not want to offend them. Based on my cultural awareness, I have no justifications whatsoever to marry the Chief's daughter instead of a lady of my own background. Please clear this confusion, and give me the right answer."

Timoli was concerned about his parents' feelings. He had no idea how to go about convincing his family. The next day, however, when he was getting ready to speak with his parents, he was surprised to notice that, all of a sudden, Timoli's parents came to approach him on their own volition. He also noticed that they were calm and relaxed. The father asked, Timoli, "can you tell us exactly how, why and when did you ever conceive the idea of proposing to Denoza?" Timoli answered to his father in few words, saying "it is the Lord, my God had shown me in my dream, and he opened the door for me to speak to Denoza, the chief's daughter. God is the one who had waved the barrier of the class status because he did not create them. In fact, Denoza and I have already met, and we have spoken to each other. Timoli's parents were really amazed, and they had their eyes wide open to hear this confirmation, because they knew that the connection between both social classes was not an easy matter.

How did you get to reach the Chief's daughter? His parents asked him. Timoli replied that God had put Nianga who happen to be Denoza's best friend on my way. This is how God had opened the door wide open for me to get in without any doubt and fear. Denoza had also introduced me to Chief Mundu and his wife. I have spoken with them as well, and they will like to meet with you on this coming Saturday evening at the Chief's residence.

His parents were actually surprised to witness the courage of their son in reaching such a higher level to establish a relationship? They suddenly stood up, and stared at each other. They began mumbling, "what a surprise!" It took them a while for both of them to digest this idea. The mother exclaimed! Timoli, do you mean that Chief Mundu and his wife want really to meet us? Timoli replied, that is correct, Mama. The Chief and his wife would like my family and me to appear on Saturday evening at his residence.

MIKWAYA AND DENOZA FAMILIES' MEETING

As Timoli's parents were getting prepared to meet Chief Mundu and his wife on the next Saturday, they started to get very nervous. They wondered what kind of questions they would be asked. On Friday evening however, the day prior to their meeting, they called Timoli, and asked him "what kind of questions did Chief Mundu and his wife asked you when you met them? Did they ask you whether or not we own any cattle, farms, sheep, goats, chickens, and ducks and so on?" Timoli replied not really, they only focused their attention on my new teaching career in the "Far Away Town."

His father reminded his wife," we must get ready to prepare questions and answers in terms of what we own and what we don't own. Let us practice tonight said Timoli's father to his wife anxiously:

He uttered,when we go to the Chief's house, if they asked us:

How many cows do you own? – We will respond in unison,

none.

If they ask us how many sheep – we will answer," Ten"

If they ask us how many goats do you have – We will reply – "seven"

If they ask us how many pigs do you own? – We will say "six"

How many ducks – we will answer "zero", and we will continue to answer zero from this point on. This was an agreement between Timoli's mother and his father prior to the meeting.

When Timoli and his parents had arrived at the Chief's residence, they were well received. Denoza was well dressed; she escorted them to meet the Chief and her mother. The Chief noticed however that they appeared very shy. They were told to be seated, and not to be afraid. Shortly, the Chief said to them. We congratulate Timoli Mikwaya, the most educated gentleman in our village. The Chief continued I attended the graduation ceremony at the Mission last Month. I saw Timoli delivering speech, and everyone was very impressed and happy about it. I just learned by my daughter Denoza that he is your son. Timoli's parents were so happy to hear the manner in which the Chief was praising their son.

At that point they started to be relaxed, whereas in t a short while they had appeared tense and frightful.

Suddenly, the Chief changed the subject and his tone of voice as well. He told Timoli now we want you to tell us the main reason that brought you and your parents here today, in front of my wife, me and my daughter Denoza? What exactly you desire to tell us at the presence of your own parents?

Please speak loud, and articulate your words the same way you did at the Mission hall, so that all of us can hear it clearly and distinctly. Chief Mundu had actually said it in such a commanding voice!

Mikwaya was a little bit nervous at first, but stood up and pronounced his words distinctly, "Chief Mundu, our own Excellent Chief of the Village, Mrs. Mundu and my beloved parents, the purpose of my visit in your home today, is to propose to your daughter Denoza, he confirmed. Timoli continued I have a deep conviction that it is the will of God for me to marry no other woman in our village but Denoza. I have been offered a teaching position at the "Far Away Town."

I have been shown several times in dream that the right spouse to accompany me there must be Denoza. Denoza told me that it was your wish for me to bring my family along so that we all can meet each other and have a further discussion regarding this matter. Timoli spoke his words humbly.

Timoli continued I am a scholar, well educated from Sowa Mission. I desire to marry a wife from my own village, especially your daughter who knows all our cultures in details.

This will help me to teach my children as well as my students. My teaching career will begin in two months. I pray to God if it is his will to allow me to get married this month, so that everything can be in readiness by then.

Chief Mundu and his wife stood up and said in unison, "Yes", we do consent. Our main reason to consent to your marriage with Denoza is the fact that you are a well known scholar of our village. We are pleased that you will be taking Denoza to "Far away Town." Denoza will be a Teacher's wife and her children will be scholars as well. Both families shook hands joyously rejoicing exceedingly for such happy ending.

However, shortly afterwards, the chief and his wife noticed that Timoli's family appeared concerned about something which they couldn't specify at first. Eventually, it has to be the dowry, the traditional wedding requirements which the groom will have to meet prior to the wedding. The Chief and his wife could feel that concern in the air. Nevertheless, Denoza's mother asked them do you have anything to say about your son's wish. Mikwaya's mother stood up, and spoke in a very nervous and frail voice,"

Yes," Chief our own concern will be in meeting the traditional marriage dowry. Our main problem is the fact that we are a modest family as you know. Chief Mundu, we have never owned any cow in our life. We were wishing that you would not consent this marriage in order to save us from embarrassments; tears were streaming down her cheeks as she started to say these words. Timoli's father shook his head, and looking at the Chief and his wife's direction then added, "Yes", Chief Mundu and Mrs. Mundu, my wife is right. It would indeed be so hard even worse for my wife and me to think about providing twenty six cows including money and the rest of the items.

As far as Timoli's parents were concerned none of the chief's daughter ever married a man from a modest family. Normally, the modest families were accustomed to just watch and observe the events from far away. Therefore they were certain that Denoza's family would dismiss their son, because the Chief and his wife knew very well that Timoli's family could never meet the dowry's obligations to both, father 's as well as mother's side of the bride.

Timoli kept quiet but devastated inside, and he wondered why did his parents have to offer this piece of private information, whereas the Chief and his wife did not ask about their possession? The Chief, his spouse and Denoza were, however, so amazed to notice how honest and humble Timoli's parents appeared to be.

The Chief and his wife did not make it difficult for Timoli's family to honor the entire dowry. Customary, to marry a chief's daughter the groom will have to offer the following items: twenty six cows, ten sheep, forty six goats, ten chickens, twelve gallons of Traditional Wine, five cases of various drinks and many other small gadgets. In the case of Timoli's family, because it was obvious that they could not afford all these items, the chief stood up and said to

Mikwaya 's family: "do not be disturbed , I am waving some requirements, and reducing the number of items you are supposed to offer me in exchange of my daughter's hand. The reason I am taking this approach is due to the fact that your son will be taking my daughter, Denoza to "Far away Town." For this reason, I am giving a special list of items designed just for Timoli Mikwaya, the most educated man in our village.

On the day of traditional wedding which will be held on the next Saturday, said Chief Mundu to Timoli's parents, "You will bring the following items only: Ten Sheep , ten goats, five pigs, six chickens, four ducks and 10 gallons of traditional Wine (known as MAN – MA-MBA). Two men's suits (one goes to the bride's uncle (Chief Mokwe) and another goes to the Father's bride (Chief Mundu). In addition, you will bring eight women's wax (high quality African women's fabric). Chief Mokwe and other judges will be notified so that they do not make it hard on you. While the judges will be calling the items to present, they will have to use the list number two that does not read: "Now present twenty six COWS", rather they will call from the list that reads: "Now present: Ten Sheep and so on."

Actually, Chief Mundu's consent for his daughter to marry Timoli was a breaking news to the entire village. People have different reaction to learn about this confirmation. They were shocked, so amazed and excited when they had been discussing the Chief's daughter's engagement with Timoli Mikwaya, a man from a modest family!

On the street, almost in every corner, one would notice individuals gathered to discuss this issue. Some people have been trying to rationalize the reason why Chief Mundu would actually consent Timoli's marriage proposal. Many people could not get it together because they have never seen any marriage being performed between any Chief's daughter and a man coming from a modest family. A lady around the corner once shouted, "I have never thought I would live to see a marriage connection between a chief's daughter and a son of a modest family." Mikwaya really made a history said neighbors. However, where would his family get the dowry from? Especially Cows, they don't own any. People made it such a big issue, and it became their concern.

Timoli's family however, considered itself to be privileged because they were given such a short list of items required for the traditional wedding dowry. Those were indeed items they were able to afford in order to allow a modest man as Timoli Mikwaya to marry Chief Mundu's daughter. According to the culture, the ancestor's law requires that there must be a cooperative action for the celebration of any family event. Prior to the celebration, the leader of the family must call for a meeting. Every family member must feel obligated to bring in its contribution. This is a family commitment where everyone's effort and love must be felt at this particular time.

Regardless how wealthy the groom's or bride's parents are, they cannot refuse the contribution of everyone else, and this is termed "A family matter," whee every family member feels connected with each other. There is no set amount required. No pressure should be put on anyone. Each person should contribute based on his or her means. The main thing is that everyone has contributed. The burden of a family must be shared with its constituents. The entire family must be mobilized to chip in, and make sure that everything goes harmoniously well so that their family could get a good reputation.

CHAPITER IV

TRADITIONAL WEDDING PREPARATION – Dress Code

Chiefs and their families were familiar with the dress code; they knew exactly what to wear on that special occasion.

Chief would wear their new Lipiah (Majestic piece of clothing designed just for chiefs to wear in the bottom and a jacket on the top, usually matching one of the three color on Lipiah) and their wives would wear a high quality Wax (high quality of African's women's material) sawn in different style according to their preferences. Their hair will be newly breaded in a majestic style. However, their head would be covered some with the same piece of their main outfit. Others would select a special silk whose color matching with the outfit. It is all a matter of taste and preference.

Mikwaya's family however had a little hard time trying to get their outfits together for such a big occasion. They were somewhat nervous because this was going to be their first association with a very high class family. Every family member was offering them a piece of an advice or suggestion about what they really should dress or how they actually should appear in order to represent their family in a respectful manner. Every family member also went out of his or her way to find a very decent suit or wax to wear so that they too could be well dressed on the wedding Day. The elderly women as well as all the young ladies were also busy trying to decide which hair style they should have their hair braided in order to appear elegant.

Cousin Lipopo, the soccer player knew how to excite all the family lards and men to make sure they are well groomed, and put on their proper attire in order to support their Scholar, Timo Mikwaya. Lipopo reminded everyone in the family especially all the youth to "remember, this is a huge event for our family. It is not that we are competing with the chief's family but it is because we do not want the audience to think that our family is not worthy to get into a close association with the chief's family.

Lipopo continued, in reality, at first all of us had wished that Chief Mundu would object Timoli's marriage proposal to his daughter in order to save a modest family like ours from pressure."

Unfortunately, Lipopo continued, Chief Mundu and his wife Kibo just fond of Timoli. Besides, based on his appearance, nobody can really turn him down. Not even the chief's daughter. Probably it is God's will since Timoli is so religious.

It is very difficult to explain the whole situation to an average person who cannot get over this shock yet. I remember Timoli repeatedly saying, "God has a Mighty Power to change any situation over night." I wish I can have faith like him, Lipopo concluded.

The simple fact that Chief Mundu has reduced the dowry, and he had given a special list of the items which needed to be called during the traditional wedding celebration, on Saturday, this fact proved that the chief and his wife are really accepting Timoli Mikwaya to become their son-in-law.

People considered this event historical. When the news first broke that a man from a modest family was proposing to the Chief's daughter, it spread in the entire village, subsequently in the nearby villages. The majority of the people expressed their feelings and comments, using the current expression of that time, which was

"Waya!!" Meaning that is a wishful thinking for Timoli Mikwaya, a guy coming from a modest family, how could he ever marry a chief's daughter! That is really a trivial nonsense!

People continued to rationalize the situation; chief Mundu worships culture and high class mannerism, and it is impossible for anyone to make him do otherwise. Further, Chief Mundu set himself too high in order to belittle himself to that point. In addition, his wife Kibo is a princess; how would they belittle themselves that far, and why would they want to associate themselves with Timoli Mikwaya's family? That is nothing but "WAYA!" People passed judgments and made awful comments concerning this matter. The majority of the people had just refused to believe it. Some of them said repeatedly," well, we will believe it only when it becomes apparent." However later on the people learned that the reason the chief had allowed his daughter to marry Timoli was because he was a scholar and a teacher, also because he was going to live in a "Far Away Town." This actually is the manner in which this situation was being justified at that particular time.

Regardless to all the "WAYA's" that went on, and all other negative statements that were made against modest family, Timo Makwaya's dream did come true. The celebration activities continued in the chief's property.

The first thing anyone would notice as soon as he enters Chief Mundu's property, is the manner in which the tables and chairs were lined up. This surely showed the place where the guests would be seating. In addition, the area where all the chiefs from different villages would be seating had been beautifully decorated, with a sign, saying,"lipiah". Further, the areas where the Judges from both parties (bride and groom) would be standing to debate the marriage dowry had been designed in a different format, usually in a circle.

SPECIAL EVENT: SATURDAY THE NUPTIAL DAY

On Saturday during marriage ceremony, the plans were about to go awry. Regardless to that special dowry list which Chief Mundu and his wife had given to Timoli Mikwaya's family in order to help alleviate the pressure of the dowry, and also to save them from embarrassment in from of the audience who had already been so critical of a modest family, the servants got thing mixed up. The judges, although had been notified that Timoli's case was completely different from the others, therefore, the judges should honor the second list and not the traditional dowry listing.

Although the Judges were well informed that Timoli's dowry list was modified in order to suit his family's need, however the servant was not cautious enough. The servant should have given the judge only the modified dowry list. Unfortunately, he gave the judges both listing, the traditional one that reads:"And now the groom's family will offer Twenty six cows", instead of reading from the modified list that reads: And now the groom's family will offer ten sheep. Timoli Mikwaya's family was made aware of this arrangement from the beginning and expected things to happen in that manner.

The judges unfortunately overlooked at that request, and had not been cautious enough in terms of selecting the correct list. They were so anxiously to begin calling the dowry successively. As soon as everyone was gathered, and the groom had been introduced to the chiefs, the judges and to the audience, four judges stepped forward on the area designed to call the list of items required to offer as dowry

The moderator, was so anxious, and picked up the traditional list instead. On the revised listing, Chief Mundu had omitted some livestock such as the offering of the twenty six cows and forty six goats. But the moderator came up, and erroneously shouted, please be quiet: We are about to call the items that the groom's family must offer in exchange to chief's daughter hand:

Number one, may the groom's family offer now," half of the twenty six cows!" The groom's family could not believe their ears, they exclaimed, WHAT! COWS! As soon as they heard the judge pronounced the word Cow! They wondered whether or not Chief Mundu had tricked them when he gave them that special dowry list? The groom's family started to shake with their eyes wide open. They were facing each other, whispering, what did the judge said "cow" but we do not have any cow. The groom's mother was frantic, and all of a sudden, she felt on the floor, and lost consciousness. The groom's father on the other hand hit the floor, the hat swung from his head, and felt on the chair. Two chairs standing nearby were pushed far away. Timoli Mikwaya ran towards his mother in order to assist her.

On the other hand, two fellows ran towards his father in order to bring him assistance as well.

All of a sudden, two servants brought some traditional medicine to have Mikwaya's mother inhaled. Shortly afterwards, she resumed her consciousness, and she was given a glass of water to drink. His father on the other hand was put back on the seated position. He was well again and was also given a glass of water to drink.

Timoli's cousin Lipopo looked straight in Timoli's eyes as to reprimand him. Didn't I warn you about this whole scenario? I surely knew something of this kind was going to happen. It was just too good to be true about that special dowry list you were so proud about. See, cousin, Chief Mundu tricked you, and fooled all of us.

On the other hand, Chief Mundu realized instinctively that there had been a mixed up in regard to the dowry listing. Therefore, he stood up, and made a quick announcement. Let me have your attention please, he said,"Which one of you gentlemen gave the Judges those dowry's lists? One of servants stood up, and replied nervously, Chief it is I who gave both lists to the Judges. Noticing such confusion that needed to settle right there and then,

Chief Mundu initiated an interruption, and immediately called the Judges. And then all of them gathered around him in order to give them a clear and quick clarification.

The conference actually lasted about five minutes. This consultation was to advise them that the servant was actually wrong. He should have given you only one special and modified list to call from. It is the list that should have read: "Now the groom's family offers their tens sheep, ten goats, etc... Chief Mundu ordered the judges to please disregard that first listing which read: "Twenty six Cows." Please remember, he said to them, "Today, we are not talking about Cows," he concluded.

In the meantime, the critics were getting excited as usual. They began whispering from left to right, "modest family should have understood this matter from the beginning. Even though this gentleman has a high level of education, nevertheless, he comes from a modest family. He should have stayed where he belongs. Whoever had told him that the dowry with the Chief's daughter can be celebrated without requesting any cow? The judges are not to blame. They are so accustomed to reading from a traditional list whose initial word begins with C- own. "The word cow is a routine, and it could not have been otherwise, concluded one of the critics, jerking and shrugging.

Chief Mundu was so courageous, he stood up, and calm everyone, and said, "I made it clear from the beginning that there is a specially dowry list that has been designed just for Timoli Mikwaya's family. I know this situation has never occurred before as far as the Chiefs' daughters' marriage proposal is concerned. Timoli Mikwaya's family is an exceptional family, he explained. This family is receiving my special treat because it has honored our Village by raising an important Scholar from this village.

This family was able to send Timoli Mikwaya to the Mission to study for such a long time. He is now the most educated gentleman in this village. This young man is so special, he said. He has been offered a Teaching job at "Far Away Town." My daughter will accompany him as his wife. Therefore, based on this reason, I am requesting for the judges to successively call the dowry items from that special list which I had authorized and designed just for the groom's family. So at this point, I would like to request that everyone 1 remains seated and quiet as the judges proceed." Everyone obeyed Chief Mundu's instructions.

The moderator actually apologized for having caused such a chaos, and ultimately, he began reading from that special list which had a very few items to offer. Apparently, the list showed that the cash requested was just in a moderate amount, compared to that of the traditional listing. Henceforth, the atmosphere became harmonious. Chief Mundu and his wife Kibo as well the bride's uncle Chief Mokwe and his wife Mikoke, all of them stood up and walked rapidly towards the groom's family at the area where they were assigned to seat.

They actually had come personally to apologize, and also to comfort and support them morally for having experienced such a temporary embarrassment. The audience was carefully watching the scene with admiration. Prince Mokwe appeared humble before the groom parents. He spoke with such respect and compassion. Apparently, the groom's family moral was restored quickly.

CELEBRATION OF TRADITIONAL WEDDING – AFTER THE DOWRY DEBATE

The traditional wedding on the bride's father side was held on Saturday afternoon, at the Chief's huge property. The celebration occurs outdoor. The dance place (cabaret) was already built in with Palm three branches attached with assorted flowers, predominantly, white flowers and African violet. This dance place called Cabaret was built for the youth and especially for the newlywed to dance. Whereas the open area was reserved, and one can easily tell at a glance that the area was indeed reserved for traditional dance because of a stack of traditional musical instruments that were at the open view.

Customarily, the traditional dance is dedicated to the elders and especially to the Chiefs and their wives. They supposed to be the ones to appear initially on the dance place as soon as the sound of the musical instrument "M'PUIT "is heard. The sound of these traditional instruments is actually so powerful that it travels miles away. At the very first sound of those musical instruments, people would stand up spontaneously with a smile in their faces, as they would walk towards the dance area. They would actually initiate dancing prior to reaching the dance floor.

On that day, there was an interesting scene to observe regarding one couple. The couple was the bride's uncle, Chief Mokwe of Zama Village and his wife Mikoke. Both, husband and wife had a remarkable figure each. Mrs. Mokwe weighed about one hundred and eighty five pounds, medium height. However, her buttocks were slightly pushed backwards. The manner in which she had been dancing, and swinging her body attracted everyone's attention. She moved one step forward, one step backward, then, she would shake both of her shoulders as well as her behind graciously at the same time. Finally, she would face her husband, Chief Mokwe, and then both would clap hands following the rhythm of Mubiri dance. Everyone enjoyed watching them dance. Chief Mokwe was remarkably handsome, six feet five tall. Spoke with such a powerful deep voice. When he spoke or laughed everyone had to look towards him. One can tell that indeed he had a royal blood in him.

FOOD PREPARATION

Regarding to the food, the Cooks knew exactly how to make a variety of Special traditional wedding dishes, and especially the famous protein dish called "NTERE DISH or mbika (pumpkin seed)" cooked or baked in different flavors namely: ntere and nko or soso, (pumpkin seed and chicken, ntere and mbisi (pumpkin seed with fish), ntere and ntab (pumpkin seed and goat meat), ntere and mikoso (pumpkin seed with Shrimp or baby shrimp), ntere and Boh (pumpkin seed with Mushroom), ntere and Makayabo (pumpkin seed with catfish), ntere and ngombe (pumpkin seed with beef) and finally ntere and bisaka (pumpkin seed with vegetable).

In addition to protein dishes, there were also cooked and baked meat (beef, pork, goat, lamb (stew and baked, fish in tomatoes sauce also baked and fried; They also cooked shrimps and baby shrimps, fried, as well as cooked in Okras. In addition, they cooked, SOSO na Mwamba (chicken in peanut butter sauce).

The farm workers had done their part, and brought in fresh fruits for desert. They also had brought in fresh vegetables and tomatoes needed for the celebration.

The cooks had prepared assorted vegetables, namely: Nkofi (collar green), Beteku-teku (Kalaloo), saka-saka (cassava leaves), epinard (spinach) and masangu (corn).

The dishes were to be served with either: Corn meal - Fufu, Millet- Cassava - Fufu, Corn-Cassava - Fufu, Rice, Green plantains, yellow plantains (Fried, boiled, and mashed) , including Mbala (Sweet Potato), Bikwa (Yam)and kwanga (baked cassava dish).

In order to accommodate every guest, dishes are cooked in different flavors based on different spices. Some food would taste mild in order to permit guests to either add hot sauce or eat it as is. Certain food would taste moderately hot, and others would taste extremely hot. Actually it all depends on the people's tastes and preferences. The main goal is to make sure that every guest had been served in a satisfactorily manner.

Concerning Beverage

The servants had also prepared beverages of different flavor, such as traditional Palm tree Wine, Coffee (strong and mild), and also assorted herb Teas as well as several big traditional ceramics bottles (called Mabungu) of Spring Water.

In regarding to Desserts

Although, Fresh fruits such as: Papaya, Mango, Banana, Orange, Tangerine, Pineapple and Mikate (sweet donut) are made available, usually people do not feel obligated to have dessert right after their big meals, but at the later time guests who desire can have it right there or they are allow to carry it home.

THE WEDDING DINER TIME

The tables were lined up outdoor along Chief Mundu's huge property. The benches were lined up along the tables as well.

Chief Mundu was seated at the head of the table and his wife Kibo was seated on his right hand. And then, Chief Mokwe was seated at the end table facing Chief Mundu and his wife Mikoke was seated at his right Hand. The rest of the Chiefs and their wives were seated around Chief Mundu and some were placed around Prince Mokwe and his wife. The Pastor and his wife were seated in the middle facing the newlywed couple.

The servants were busy, actively bringing food from the Kitchen, when all of a sudden, there was an announcement, and "Everyone please keep silence!" The Pastor has arrived! The Pastor from the local church was invited to bless the food and had to partake the diner as well. Everyone was to remain silence. The Pastor had a Bible in his hand, and he read one verse of the scripture. Then, invited people to be in a receptive position, suddenly he started to pray. The prayer was specific and the words were appropriate with the wedding occasion. It was just quite a propos, and the atmosphere was just harmonious.

The servants began actively serving. They were just into their duties that one of them could not quite remember that the

Pastor and his wife do not drink any types of Wine, because it contains alcohol in it.

The servant poured a glass of wine, and placed it next to the Pastor; and he poured another glass of wine then placed it next to his wife. The Pastor's wife noticed it, and right away whispered in her husband's ear, I wonder why the servant is serving us wine? Doesn't he know that we are religious people and that we are not supposed to drink alcohol?

The Pastor replied that I am pretty sure that he is innocent; I do not believe that this young man did it intentionally in order to test us or to tempt us. As they were carrying on that small discussion about the wine, Denoza and Timoli overheard the conversation. Then Denoza raised her hand toward the servant, and then right away, one of the servants rushed towards her. Denoza told him silently, to remove the glass of wine that was placed next to the Pastor and also the one next to his wife. She added and explained to him that "The Pastor and his wife are the servants of God, and therefore they do not drink wine." She continued, kindly ask them what would they prefer to drink coffee, tea or spring water?

The servant approached the Pastor and his wife, he was very apologetic. He then asked their preferences. The Pastor chose to drink coffee, and his wife had preferred to drink "Bulukutu" herb tea because she adored the aroma of "Bulukutu herb tea."

After the traditional wedding, the couple had requested a religious wedding prior to departure to the "Far Away Town." The local church was packed with different guests that day. The people who had come late, had eventual no seats; they were standing out of the church. Fortunately, the church windows were left open. Many people took watching the ceremony through the windows.

The choir sang joyously, enthusiastically lovely songs. The choir director was well fond of by the congregation. He knew how to swing with those beautiful melodies. Especially when the choir began singing the famous wedding song which reminds the bride and the groom that this was their "***Big Day***" the day which you have both decided to become husband and wife in the eyes of God, in the eyes of all the Chiefs as well as in the eyes of all who have gathered here.

May you always remember the following words?

> *Denoza, Denoza is your wife- Is your wife (2 xs)*
>
> *Henceforth she is your real spouse – accept her as your*
>
> *spouse and remain faithful.*
>
> *Timoli, Timoli is your husband –Is your husband (2x)*
>
> *Henceforth he is your real husband – accept him as your husband and remain faithful.*

Everyone was so eager that the whole congregation could not help singing along with the choir. The church was shaken with joy and enthusiasm. People concluded that the celebration of traditional marriage was beautiful however, the celebration of the religious marriage was spectacular; the air was filled with happiness and joy.

Finally both family members were overwhelmed with joy, and they started to hug each other; the barriers which once stood between both families were broken. Mutual respect was established with such relaxed atmosphere.

The critics however continue to be amazed to witness that special event. Different individuals had mixed feelings in regard to such unusual event. They could not actually digest the fact that a man from a modest family had been able to marry Chief Mundu's daughter! Chief Mundu, a man who presented himself with full dignity.

People considered Timoli Mikwaya to be an exceptional man, courageous and fearless. Some people stated that Mikwaya was extremely lucky to become a Chief Mundu's son-in –law. Whereas other people could not imagine how in the world did Mikwaya manage to connect with the Chief's daughter? People were just puzzled. They couldn't help wondering the how and when and under which circumstance could this gentleman bridge the gap between the chief's world and the modest world? People went on digging and digging the missing piece.

CHAPTER V

NEWLYWED'S COUNSELING SESSION PRIOR TO DEPARTURE

Nevertheless, Denoza and Timoli were happily married. Three days after the wedding ceremony they started to prepare for traveling to "Far Away Town", where Timoli was stationed in order to begin his new teaching career.

Both the groom and the bride's families were very knowledgeable of their traditions, and practiced the culture well. Based on the culture, the newlywed must undergo a series of counseling with their folks prior to departure, and never after their departure. Each family took its full responsibilities to seat with their child. The newlywed should be made aware of what is permissible and what is not permissible in the marriage. The culture states, "Parents must give advice to their children prior to going out in order to prevent the worse. Never give advice after the child has already gone out; this would be too late because there would be no powerful statement from the parents which could help the child to refrain from taking a wrong action."

The evening prior to departure to "Far Away Town", Timoli's parents call him privately for counseling. His father started first saying, "my son, tomorrow you will be departing from our village to the Far Away Town. Remember son, now you are a married man. When the judges had called the wedding requirements from that list, so do remember those items that we, the family had offered, they truly represent a Very Big Commitment.

You cannot overlook at the wedding dowry. Those items actually mean that you're vowed to Chief Mundu and his wife, as well as their entire family, and especially to the prince, Chief Mokwe, Denoza's uncle. Further, you vowed to God and to us, your father, your mother and your entire family. Please do not forget these things. You stated with all you are and have that I, Timoli Mikwaya, vow to take care of my wife Denoza Mundu, and that I will protect her with God's guidance.

Furthermore, I will sacrifice my own life in order to safe my wife's life if need be; and no matter what happens between and around us, I will stood for Denoza. Do you recall what you had said in front of the judges and everybody else, son? Timoli's father asked? Because Timoli had always been so humble in front of his folks, so with all his respect Timoli meekly replied, Papa, thank you so much for reminding me about our precious culture. Truly, I do understand, and I shall recall it very well. Then, he continued saying, "I must promise you, Papa that I shall recall your advice from now henceforth, there is no doubt about it. I will never take it lightly as long as I shall live!"

Further came his mother's turn to speak, and she said, "Timoli my son, remember this, "your wife is a female like me, your Mama. The same respect you give me, it is the same respect you will show your wife. Never curse her parents regardless of the situation which may cause you to lose your temper. Should any misunderstanding occur between husband and wife, please, son, do not lift your hand to beat your wife? Do you hear me, son? Do not scream, but call her privately and talk to her in a calm and moderate tone of voice." Remember, she insisted, "women do not appreciate roaring voice, because it makes the matter worse, especially when it causes a woman to cry."

In addition, his mother said, "A good man must control his speech; please remember to refrain from pronouncing words which may irritate your spouse, because the sound of an unkind word causes pain in the heart, and it hurts just like pepper. Beware my son, and remember that if your wife is unhappy, you the man, will be miserable regardless of your appearance or your wealth. This is actually a secret I am revealing to you today, and you ought to remember it always.

Do you understand my son?" Timoli, replied with deep appreciation to his mother, "Yes" Mama, I do. Mama, he added, I thank you for reminding me of our sacred culture. I understand and I shall act as you have advised me. Mikwaya's mother said, "Respect" is the key word, my son; make sure you remember this word," his mother concluded as she blessed him, saying, go in peace and be merry.

On the other hand, Chief Mundu and his wife Kibo called their daughter Denoza, privately as well, and Chief Mundu began saying, "Denoza my beloved daughter, tomorrow you and your husband will be departing from our village. Remember you are now a married woman. You will carry yourself as a married woman. Your husband is the boss in your house, and you must not command him. However you may advise him, the same way your mother does with me. Obviously, our culture requires that you, as a woman to be submissive to your husband. Make sure you fix your house well. Please, never tell your husband that in my parents' house I was not doing this and that, and the other thing. It has been your personal decision to marry a man who is not from our family status.

You will have to try to do all he household tasks by yourself. This is how women in modest families act. However, while you are there, should situations become overwhelmed for you, in that case, do not hesitate to write us and seek for help. We will send you one of the servants to help you out. However before you do that you must remember that you are a married woman at the present time, and you should always ask the permission of your spouse prior to taking any action including asking help from us.

Chief Mundu Continued, Denoza your duty as a married woman is to cook for your husband, and put the food on the table on time. Keep harmony around the house, no matter what goes on around you. Do you notice how your mother treats me? She is a princess, she is also an heiress but she has never made a big issue or sings about her royal blood because she knows quite well that I am aware of her root.

Your mother knows that having a royal blood should not be a weapon to fight with her husband. At the same time the husband should not ignore his wife's root either; it is quite natural to voice it only whenever people attempt to mistreat you. You must show respect to your husband because he already knows that you have a royal blood in your veins. Above all, it is preferable that you do not form the habit of reminding him that he is from a modest family. That surely would be an offense to him, and this would not bring any happiness in your marriage. Remember always, to be courteous to your husband, in this way God can give you blessed children. You will be going to "Far Away Town" with my blessing, her father concluded. Denoza replied, Papa I thank you for your wise advice. I promise to remember everything you have just told me.

Then Denoza's mother stood up and said to her, "Denoza, my daughter, you know how much I love you. There is nothing that you have not received from your father and me, whenever you needed it. Remember therefore that you have a royal blood, and we are a well to do family. We have always had servants in this house prior to your birth. Henceforward, remember your life has changed, now. Timoli is taking you to a "Far away Town," and we do not know whether or not your spouse would be able to afford a domestic to help you out. However, you are to remember that currently, you are a married woman. You opted to marry Timoli Mikwaya, and he is from a modest family. You will therefore begin taking initiative in managing your household.

You have always been aware of his social status; therefore, no matter what happens in your daily activities, I beg you keep calm, and do not act arrogant to your husband, never. You must be cautious, never to say irritating words to your husband. You should try to show the same respect and obedience to your spouse as you always show them to your father and me.

The princess continued, Denoza, my dear daughter, know exactly who are your parents, and what they own. Therefore, you must be so careful, not to use bad expressions in the usage of your daily language which would disdain his family, and that could also disrupt your marriage. Actually, the following are the things you should avoid saying to your spouse, "I cannot listen to you; I am a Chief's daughter, and in my parents' home I am not accustomed to perform such and such duties, because I have always been serviced by my parents' servants. Due to the fact that you came from a modest home, you can serve yourself.

My daughter, remember that saying such irritating things would be disrespectful to your husband, as well as to our culture. So, learn to act as a dove, humble and be submissive, and strive in creating a harmonious family relationship.

Further know that you are representing me, your mother. The princess, continued, also remember that a mother, always gets the credit for any good action that her married daughter does for her spouse. I shall look forward to receiving that credit. She looked straight at her mother and replied calmly, Mama, "I thank you for all your advices and the wisdom associated to them. I promise you shall receive the credit you deserve."

In addition, the princess said "it is preferably to do things that are pleasing to your husband, because they will make him happy. However, do not be afraid of him; rather make your husband your best friend. Speaking politely to each other brings happiness. When you talk to your spouse calmly, nicely, courteously, your husband will never be furious regardless to the situation. This is the secret to save a marriage. "LUZITU" or Respect is a Key word," my Daughter. Did I make myself clear?

This is how our culture really demands, my daughter, we are required to give advice to the newlywed individuals prior to entering in their marriage life.. Denoza thanked her mother as well, and added, Mama and Papa, I am glad that you both are my parents who carry valuable cultural information, which is worthy to remember in order to build a society which will reflect our ancestors' integrity. I shall recall your advice for eternity. Her mother said to her, my daughter may all my blessings go with you! We shall pray so that God send you special children. Go in peace, she added, hugging her.

The day of their departure to the "Far Away Town," the chief offered a Truck loaded with all the necessary items needed for Denoza and her husband to start a new family. The Chief selected the best truck driver to escort Timoli and Denoza to a Far Away Town. Both Timoli and Denoza were seated in the front seat next to the driver, whereas the two other men, known as Chief's Mundu's servants were seated behind with all the wedding gifts. They drove for twelve hours, and finally they arrived at their new home. Neighbors were expecting their arrival.

They had wished them a warm welcome. Denoza and Timoli noticed that their neighbors were extremely kind to them. Timoli's job offered them a lovely three bed room's home, surrounded by a big garden. They noticed that there were the following fruit trees in the garden: one avocado tree, one mango tree and three banana trees in their backyard. On the left side of their home stood two palm trees, and around the house were beautiful flowers, including African violet. Further, on the extreme right there stood one orange tree by itself.

Denoza loved their home very much. All those fruit trees reminded her of the trees located in her parents' property in the village. She could hardly believe that she had become Mrs. Mikwaya, the man whom she looked down, and she wouldn't dare to look at, even for a second. She started to realize however that her husband really was not a religious man but a sincere spiritual man. She remembered that only God alone could have made this situation possible. Furthermore, she also recalled how stern her mother had been in terms of maintaining her royal blood identity. In addition, she thought about how reluctant her further had been at first, to think about the fact that a man from a modest family was daring to propose to a Chief's daughter.

She concluded however that God alone has the power to change things around at any time. Here I am today, she concluded; people are now addressing me as Mrs. Mikwaya, a teacher's wife, she added. Denoza, started to realize the magnitude of a "Being, called God!" He indeed has a Mighty Power to actually break the barriers, and He did.

CHAPITER VI

DENOZA CONCEIVED A CHILD - DISMISSED THEIR SERVANTS

The servants who had accompanied them to Town remained with them for six months in order to help out around the house. Chief Mundu ordered them to stay with them for at least one year until they are settled down. However, six months later, Denoza conceived. The culture also recommends that the first pregnancy should not be announced. It should remain a secret to the family member until the child is born. The reason for this is to prevent miscarriage, caused by evil spirit or jealous people or enemies.

Therefore, Denoza and Timoli, discussed the situation, and decided to let the servants go back to the village to prevent them from announcing the conception of her pregnancy.

On a Wednesday evening, Denoza and Timoli decided to have a family meeting with the servants. At first they actually praised them for every good thing which both had done for them. They expressed their sincere grateful for the excellent service they had rendered them thus far. However, they said, "We are now settled down. We feel confident that we can manage our household without aid. Therefore we would like to offer you these gifts of appreciation. You now can return to the village and report to Chief Mundu for further assignments. So, both servants returned to the village in order to resume their routine at Chief Mundu's residence. They had no slightest idea that Denoza had conceived.

Otherwise, that would have been the first thing the servants would have announced as soon as they had arrived in the village. They would have used the famous expression used to refer to a pregnant woman who is still expecting to give birth, "***She is on a high level currently***", meaning she is pregnant.

"*She has not come down yet,*" this means that she has not given birth yet. These subtle terminologies are used in the attempt to protect pregnant woman. This implies that 'THE *WOMAN'LIFE IS AT RISK WHEN SHE IS PREGNANT*, anything could happen. Therefore people talked about this subject with some sort of concern. However when she gives birth, the joyous expression used is "*SHE HAS COME DOWN NOW*"!!

When servants returned to the village, they were asked how Denoza and her spouse were doing. The servants simply replied that they are doing fantastic. The husband goes to work every morning and Denoza stay home keeping busy. She had been making dresses and camisoles for the neighbors and their children. The neighbors are so eager to notice that Denoza is an excellent dress maker. Chief Mundu, his wife and his entire family were rejoicing to hear such good news with a smile.

TIMO MIKWAYA (KAMINA)'S BIRTH

Nine months later, a baby boy was born. When Chief Mundu, his wife and family heard about the news, they shared it with the uncle, prince Mokwe, Chief of the Zama village. There was a big celebration in the village, first; and then both, Chief Mundu, his wife and Chief Mokwe along with his wife decided to came to the" Far Away Town" to pay a visit to the new born, their grandson. They brought money and a truck full of food and livestock to honor the baby.

Chief Mundu and his wife returned the servants back to the Far Away Town, in order to help Denoza and the baby. Subsequently, friends and cousins started to come to bring their money and their gifts as well. They named the child Timo Mikwaya. Later on, because of his height, the child was known also as "KAMINA."Coming from a small area, both Denoza and Mikwaya were born from families which have nothing but tall people. They have never heard or seen a small person (called Kamina or a midget). They have however heard of pigmies tribes living in the Equatorial forest, but never actually seen any of them in physical and tangible form.

The news about a baby being a small man was disturbing to both family members.Chief Mundu was a brother-in–law of Prince Mokwe of Zama village, and they had always kept in close association. Further, both of them were very wealthy.

When Timo was first born, both of his grandparents and granduncle on his mother's side were very excited. However, they grew upset shortly after they were told that Timo was a mysterious child and he has a birth defect, a height problem. Both Chiefs became actually speechless. The first thing that had gone in their mind was "probably our ancestors are not pleased with us for allowing Denoza to marry out of the royal blood?" Could that be a curse or a punishment from God, they continued to speculate? What action should we take? They wondered. One of them hypothesized probably we should return the dowry all together, and get Denoza out of Timoli Mikwaya's house.

Impulsively, Chief Mundu recalled what Mr. Mikwaya had first told him when he was attempting to propose to Denoza. He had said that, "God had revealed to me that Denoza will be my beloved wife and that she and I will give birth to a gifted child; and that that boy will be so popular."

Chief Mokwe was never made aware of that dream, and he questioned seriously. Chief Mokwe concluded that dream could actually be true, because from the beginning of Timoli and Denoza relationship, I had not felt any slightest resistance which I would have normally felt under such circumstance. Actually, due to Timoli Makwaya's social status, many people in Zama village had expected me to oppose his marriage proposal to my niece Denoza who has royal blood in her vein, on an instance. However, I could not dare to oppose to it. The Pastor had told us the other day that God always does what God wants to do at any time because He controls *the whole wide world*. I have been thinking about that Pastor's statement, and I think he might be right about it, concluded Chief Mokwe, who had some degree of God's fear and his Mighty Power.

Both family members decided to wait and see what will happen in the near future. However, deep down they were still concerned, especially when they learned that the child was denied school admission several times due to his small height. All the family members become disturbed and were very concerned about this fact. In fact, none of them had an exact answer to this seeming dilemma.

CHAPITER VII

KAMINA'S CHILDHOOD EXPERIENCE – WITH HIS MOTHER

The little boy was so handsome, bright and alert, however after four years the child seemed not to grow in height as a normal child would. He was however a very healthy boy, courageous, strong and happy. His height became a great concern to both parents. They wondered what seems to be the problem, and why in the world that stops this child from growing. The child has now reached four years old. Parents wanted to send him to school, but were afraid to do so, because he appeared too short. Neighbors, who had never seen a midget before, realized that the child should be taken to the doctor. Everyone was frantic, there is definitely something wrong with this child, concluded everyone around them. Although, he was too little for his height, he appeared to be a healthy child, with very sharp eyes.

Both Mr. and Mrs. Mikwaya took their son to a local doctor; the doctor examined him and explained to the parents that the child will probably grow a little bit more but not too much.

However, he will just remain a little guy, no more than one foot and few inches. The doctor assured them that, the most important thing is the fact that the child was healthy, strong, and courageous and in addition, he has heavy bones. Both husband and wife started to wonder. The child will be a little guy! This is absurd, they said to each other, a little man! What is that supposed to mean for our child? He probably will pull up some more but will not reach normal height, the doctor replied.

The doctor understood their concerns very well, because in the area where they came from there has never been any midget. The doctor continued, I understand your concern, I know that in this country it is very seldom for people to give birth to little people, but in many other countries that I have visited there are plenty of them leading a normal life.

From that time henceforth, the child's parents were still concerned. The mother had formed the habit of measuring the child every other day to see whether or not he has grown a little. She decided to feed him varieties of nutritious food including the kings' dishes.

This was in the attempt to make him grow taller than what was predicted. Unfortunately he grew only about 50 inches more from his previous height. He measured one foot and halt tall only. Due to the fact that the child was not growing at all, the mother became depressed. She grew bitter.

She was convinced that Timo will never get any education because of his height, and he probably will continue to be a burden on his mother for the rest of his life. Therefore, his mother began to anticipate that the only alternative would be to send him to the village, either to his grandparents, Chief Mundu or to his granduncle Prince Mokwe of Zama village. She was aware of the child's grandparents and his granduncle loved him dearly regardless to his small height, because he was outspoken, happy and also a loving child.

Both his grandfather and his granduncle had repeatedly promised him to be their heir, because they had noticed the strength and the courage Timo had always exhibited around them.

Timo's mother believed that by being around them, he would be trained how to manage his heritage, and how to deal with servants and the farms workers. Especially, he will also learn how the buvin (cowboy) manage the cattle. Further, his mother said to herself, he will have to also know where does the buvin feed the cows, and when does he walk them down the hill to the river in order to drink water. Denoza had some consolation to remember that even though, the society may treat her son with disdain, at least Timo will inherit his grandparents and granduncle wealth, and he can still maintain his high rank, and continue to gain respect.

However, the mother grew still bitter every time she looked at her son, "Timo Mikwaya, Jr." Denoza however had formed the habit of talking to her son every morning, as soon as her husband leaves for work. She would call her son Timo, and would ask him to stand before her. And then, she would have him stand on a small stool, and showing him a tape measure. Denoza would actually tell her son "Timo I will start measuring you on a regular basis. I would like to notice an increment in your height, every time I measure you." She would also order him to listen to her carefully.

The child would be staring at her quietly. And then she would start telling the child things such as:

Timo my child, you are so handsome like your father. I want you also to be tall like him. I come from a very high class family. My mother is a princess. My uncle Mokwe is a prince, he is handsome and tall. I have a royal blood in me, and my parents are well known individuals. Your grand-father, Chief Mundu is a tall man so is your granduncle Mokwe. They would be happy and proud to see my son growing tall like the rest of the children do. Timo, how do you want me to introduce you to such a high class family, if you refuse to grow? The poor child will be facing his mother with such a fearful look, and he would appear to actually cry due for being reprimanded for the cause that the child had not control over.

Denoza would order the child to observe his little friend, called Ebalo. In addition, she would say to Timo see, Ebalo is two years younger than you. Do you notice how tall he has grown? I want you also to grow tall, so that you can have a chance to go to school; and become a successful man.

Denoza would touch the child's front head, and say to him, "Timo because the world is selfish, and it is full of injustice, and therefore, in order for you to be admitted in school, you must reach the height that is required by the school administrator. Last year, because of your height, you were left behind. All the neighbors' kids were admitted in school because they met the height required. You were measured and did not meet the requirement. The school administrator said you are too short to start school. So please try to grow so that you can be admitted to school next year, and become somebody one day in life.

Denoza continued, Timo if you don't grow, you will never go to school, and if you do not go to school, nobody will dare to give you a decent job in Town. People will be looking down at you, "what can a small man do in this world? No one would even believe that your mother has a royal blood, and that you, "KAMINA" is a descendant of a royal family. You probably will wind up getting a one to two days job if any will ever be available. Usually, even that kind of work, the boss would prefer a tall man who could run quickly and have the job done in a second.

You wouldn't want to be called a turtle, would you? Timo shook his head, meaning no. She continued, well, that is why you must grow taller.

Denoza never stop talking to the child about this issue; she continued, Timo, you are being well fed, all the assorted food, even the king's dishes (corn, pumpkin seed, fish, chicken, meat, vegetable and fruits (Pineapple, orange, mango, papaya and banana), I have been feeding you all these things, don't I? Timo replied with a fearful look in his face by nodding his head, meaning, yes. Denoza looked at the child's face and asked **him,** Timo, now you tell me why aren't you growing? Don't you want to become a school teacher like your Papa? See, your Papa is a tall man, and his teachers showed him respect because of his height, besides, he is intelligent and handsome like you. You are very handsome; Timo but you are just too short "KAMINA", that is not good! Please pull up some more to highlight your beauty, son!

I have exhausted every kind of foods in the attempt to help you grow. Timo, she said, know that the reason I feed you so well is because you must grow and reach the height the school system requires here in order for you to be admitted.

The mother continued, Timo, the school administrator will be soon visiting different houses with a tape measure in order to determine whether or not you have reached the height to begin school. 'KAMINA" is not an acceptable terminology; how could you be accepted in school? You witnessed, last year you were not eligible. You were left behind. All the neighbors' kids, your friends are now going to school. Do you see how bored you appear to be behind? All day you have no one to play with after you have done your father's home works and after you have finished drawing different fruits in the garden which is very good.

However, Timo you will still need to attend school in order to learn more. Timo, your mama is concerned; it is sad because no school administrator would ever want to admit you in school with your height. I am afraid that you will be left behind again this coming year, because you are not getting any taller. You are just too Kamina (little). The mother continued to lecture Timo, Your ancestors were tall, majestic, but which world were you originated? In my entire family men are over six feet tall, in your father's side likewise.

Timo what seem to be wrong with your height? Why aren't growing? Every child of your age is twice your height!

The child had eventually no answer to these problems. Timo, the poor child would be staring at his mother, twisting his lower lip with his right hand, and sometimes crying. The other times, Timo would have his left index between his teeth, swinging from left to right while his mother will be talking to him. Then, the mother would give a child a dirty look, and one day she even try to hit him with a tape measure, fortunately it fell few steps from Timo. Finally in order to satisfy her frustration Timo's mother had formed the habit of singing a little unkind song entitled, "Kamina-Kamina" which signified (Shorty, Shorty, like a small like a head of mushroom) *to him.*

> *"KAMINA – KAMINA, ANAL LEY, TO- LA –MAN*
> *"KAMIN -KAMIN, ANA LEY, TO LA MAN*
> *"KAMIN -KAMIN, ANA LEY, TO LA MAN –EH....NIA MA-NDI*
> *EH EH, MBUR-A –MA-BWA I-WA (3X)*

The meaning of this song is "too short, too short, and too short just like a small pumpkin.

Stack of food will be exhausted, but Timo is not budging to grow, what is this?

When this poor child would hear his mother's criticism, screaming and yelling Timo would start crying, sometimes, he would refuse to eat because he would be so upset to see her mom worried about his height. The child had always wished his father would arrive quickly from work, because during this time, the mother would not dare to abuse him for she knew his father loved him dearly regardless of his height; he always spoke positive things about him, and they were very close together. His father had often referred to his early dream prior to his birth. He knew that the child had a special mission to accomplish in his life time. Whatever that mission was God alone knew it. Therefore the father treated Timo with a lot of love and respect. The child felt that love, and responded to it.

Timo knew around what time his father was arriving home from work, and he had formed the habit of seating in the chair near the doorway awaiting his father's arrival. Sometimes he would be just standing at the dooryard to run toward his daddy, and his father would run towards Timo, and both would meet half way, and then father and son would hug each other joyously. Timo would hug his father by his legs at the level of his height. Then his father would bend to pick him up and kiss him. The child was aware of the degree of his father's love, eventually it was reciprocal.

Mr. Mikwaya had formed the habit of saying to his son, "how are you doing my prince?" Timo had such a lovely face and smile. Whenever he was around his father, he would stay away from his mother completely. Both parents started noticing this fact. Finally, the mother began to worry, saying to her husband, it seems as though Timo hates me? I do not know what happens between you two at my absence, replied the husband. You should remember that children are very sensitive. They actually would pick up good vibrations immediately and would be attached to whomever producing it. At the same time, children can also feel bad vibrations, and then they would also respond accordingly. You must therefore be very careful, Denoza when you are dealing with this child.

However one day, Timo was playing in the backyard, then he started to hum his mother 'song involuntarily, he was so bright, and had a very clear speech.

He knew how to articulate the words well. Spontaneously, he stopped humming and began completely voicing the words of the lyrics:

> *KAMINA, KAMINA, ANALEY TO-LA-MAN (2 X)*
>
> *KAMINA, KAMINA ANALEY TO-LA-MAN (2 X)*
>
> *N I-A- MA-NDI, EH, E h*
>
> *MBURA – MA – BWO - IWA (3X).*

(The song meant: Too short, too short like a small pumpkin)

(A stack of food would be just exhausted, feeding Timo)-

Regardless to the variety of this food, Timo just remains

a "KAMINA." He refuses to grow tall.

His father, Mr. Mikwaya heard the song, he was so surprised and almost hurt.

Timo's father became alert, and he wondered, where could he have learned those abusive words? He was deeply disturbed, and felt so sad when facing "Kamina." He realized that his wife, Denoza must have been expressing her frustration directly at the child. Apparently, she is losing her control.

He began talking to himself. He became very curious, and wanted to really unveil this seeming mystery. Although, he had suspected that those words were originated from the child's mother. He decided somehow to call the child, and questioned him privately. My little prince, his father asked him, tell me where did you actually learn this complicated song?

To answer this question, at first the child was shy. For the first time, the father had noticed that Timo acted with this bashful attitude towards him. Timo did not respond right away. He faced the floor instead of facing his father as usual, and then he began answering, as he was swinging from left to right. He was repeating his father's question, "where did I learn the song, the song, the ,"The father told Timo, let us take a walk in the garden. Timo was happy that his father diverted the conversation, and they took a walk. And, then they stood under an avocado tree.

All of a sudden, Timo noticed one big avocado, hanging as though it was going to fall down. He asked his father, Papa, can we pick this avocado? His father replied, yes indeed, it has been ripped, and therefore they picked it up from the tree. Timo was eager to hold it in his hands.

However, Mr. Mikwaya was determined to know the truth about the origin of this song. He then resumed the question. Timo, my prince, tell me where did you learn "Kamina" song from? Timo holding the fruit in his hands, again started to look *downward and answered that "this is mama's song. Mama sings this song to* me every day when you go to work. First of all, she begins by measuring my height with her tape measure, and then she yells at me saying "why aren't you growing Timo? The child said it with the same authoritative tone of voice as his mother would sound. At this point, his father was convinced that indeed his wife was giving the child a hard time behind his back. Then Timo continued, papa, afterwards, mama then sings to me. This is how I know this song, because I hear it every day from Mama. His father asked the child did you mother explain to you the meaning of this song? Timo answered, yes, she always does.

Mama said that in our language KAMINA means "Tiny". His father felt very embarrassed, and he did not know how to go about counseling the child. Mikwaya asked the child again do you like this song. No, he replied; then why are you singing it, he asked him. The child shrugged, and replied, I don't know. I don't like it because mama gets very upset with me. Then I cry, and sometimes

Mama also cries because I am not growing like my neighbor. Then we both cry sometimes. Mama always tells me why don't I grow tall like you, Papa, and like my grandpa, Chief Mundu or like my granduncle Chief Mokwe.

The child continued, Papa, I like when I see you coming from work. I like it very much because mama won't sing this song before you. She is afraid of you. Why, then are you singing it? The father asked. Timo became so shy, and he turned his face on his right side. Today, he said, mama had measured me, and she said that from last week I only grew one inch. She wants me to grow more. She promised to feed me tomorrow one big piece of Papaya fruit. Mama also said that I will have to finish a chunk of Pineapple. His father said," what!" You will have to finish that big piece of Pineapple?

Mr. Mikwaya was amazed to hear this statement, because those are actually huge pineapple which would weigh about six to ten pounds. They come from Prince Mokwe farms. They are thick and juicy.

The plantation is around the water the area, and it produces huge, sweet and juicy pineapple. Unless it was some sort of punishment, normally the child cannot finish such a huge piece of pineapple by himself at once.

Timo continued, mama also said to me that from now on, the servant Mabula would make sure that I eat four oranges and two bananas per day. She also asked me which NTERE DISH I would like to eat tomorrow. His father asked him, and then which one did you select? The child eagerly answered, I told mama, I would like to eat "NTERE and MIKOSO" (pumpkin seed with baby shrimp) with mashed plantains. Yesterday I ate ntere and mbisi (Pumpkin seed and Fish). Timo has two favorite ntere flavors, there were: ntere and mbisi and ntere and mikoso. He could eat ntere and mikoso and ntere and mbisi every day if he could but Mama would never allow it. Timo's eating habit became some sort of joke to those around him.

In fact, everyone knew that if you ask Timo what food he would like to eat? He definitely will answer, "oh, ntere and mbisi, or ntere and mikoso."

The baking of these dishes has always been done locally. The intere dough combined with its ingredients had to be wrapped in special leaves, called, "nzombi leaves", then baked it locally. Those special leaves had an aftereffect aroma which makes the food tastes delicious. Nzombi leaves also are used by traditional artists in certain areas, in order to create special containers of various shapes, called "BIPUKU" which are used to conserve dried NTERE (pumpkin seeds) in order to keep it fresh. Since Timo's grandparents and granduncle became aware that Timo adored intere dishes, they made sure to forward at least four "BIPUKU of intere" to "Far away Town" for their grandson Timo who was so appreciative to them.

Mr. Mikwaya became irritated inside of himself for noticing his wife's peculiar behavior towards his son. He said to himself, Denoza is really exaggerating. She did not seem to realize that the child's feelings were being hurt, because he is a human being regardless to his little height.

His first reaction was to scream at her. However, he had remembered his parents' advice, and especially his mother; my mother told me, "never screamed at your spouse, no matter what happens between you. Do not cause your wife to cry." Prior to having a talk with his wife, Timoli Mikwaya opted to spend time for prayer. Prior to beginning his prayers, he thanked God for giving him a healthy, bright, alert and intelligent child.

Then he told God, "My wife, God as you can see is concerned about the future of our son. His education as well as his place in the society, but I trust that you know more about this child than we do. Please come forth and you speak through me, as I speak to Denoza at our appointed time regarding Timo tonight". Two days after his conversation with his son Timo, and after his communication with his God, Mr. Mikwaya finally decided to call his wife Denoza in order to verify their son's statement. He did it in such a calmly fashion. Timoli had noticed that Denoza was cooperative, she actually acknowledged it. Timoli Mikwaya said to his wife, I would appreciate it very much if you could stop abusing the child in this manner.

Those words are too strong for his brains to absorb. Please stop saying unkind things to Timo any longer, because he is too young, and he might ultimately lose his self-esteem.

If the child starst becoming fearful and resentful towards his own mother, this could cause a serious problem indeed in the family, the husband said. He continued this child could have been given some special gifts from God and because of the daily criticism you have been addressing him, this could actually cause a mental block to him, and hinder his divine gifts from manifesting, he said to her.

The wife attempted to defend herself, saying who ever told you that I criticize the child? The husband tried to explain to his wife, saying: Denoza, you know that I teach Timo every evening. You have noticed how bright this child is. You will be surprised to know that Timo had actually memorized all those words in "KAMINA lyrics" the negative song that you have been singing to him, everyday, while I am at work. He knows it well. Denoza it is really pathetic for this poor child.

Denoza was therefore embarrassed; nevertheless, she wanted to make sure that Timo had actually memorized the lyrics. Apparently, she was still on a defensive side. She asked her husband, which words of the lyrics Timo had actually pronounced. Her husband replied, Denoza negative words such as *"KAMINA-*

KAMINIA ANA LEY TO-LA-MAN! The child's mother was so surprised; do you really mean that this child had actually memorized the lyrics? She exclaimed! Mikwaya answered to his spouse that, "didn't I tell you that this child is exceptionally intelligent?" You noticed that I have been teaching him every evening, therefore, I had already evaluated him. I can confirm that Timo is actually a fast learner, so please select the words to address him.

He continued both of us believe in God, Denoza why don't we just trust in him? God works mysteriously, as we have learned it. God may use Timo in a strange way. You never can tell what the future will bring to this child. We cannot start abusing him because of his height. Denoza, replied to her husband, well, that would be the day; I would like to see it. I am just frustrated to see how short he is; there is no indication that he is growing at all.

How can God ever use him? Unless he grows taller who ever would want to give him any type of responsibility in his life? Apparently, Timo's mother had a negative attitude towards the child.

CHAPITER VIII

KAMINA VANISHED FROM SIGHT

One Monday morning, the child was observing a group of his little friends as they were going to school. Timo knew that he will be left behind alone, and no one to play with during that time until later afternoon, when his friends will come out of school. He had formed the habit of walking around the garden, and most of the time Timo used to sit under any selected fruit trees in the garden. He used to carry with a sheet of paper and a pencil in his hand in order to draw any fruit of his choice.

That was one of his daily hobbies, besides from doing his daily homework from his father instruction. Sometimes he would draw an avocado, and another time, he would draw a banana; and some other time he would draw a tree with fruits hanging in the branches. His drawings were the first things that Timo used to present to his father as soon as he came back home from work. His father rejoiced exceedingly to receive his son's daily creativity. He was very encouraging of his son.

One day however, Timo was walking in his backyard, all of a sudden he noticed a big bird flying from the opposite direction and then finally, the bird stood on the palm tree facing the child. Timo was so impressed to see such a big bird. That scene coincided with the lesson he had just received from his father few days ago about the birds, their eggs and their nests. Then Timo stood immovable observing the actions of that bird. The big bird's movement was a little bit too strong on the palm tree that it had caused the nest to fall down, few steps away from Timo's feet. Timo took a deep interest when he had noticed a baby bird coming out of that nest. The baby bird appeared so strange. Apparently, it did not have sprouting wings to fly away. Timo noticed that the baby bird just had tiny small feathers on his wings, and it could not fly away

Timo noticed also that instead of flying the baby bird was walking on its tiny legs, and trying to run towards the dense flowers located at the entrance of the hollow; the groove was created by a palm tree logs which had been lying over another log that was previously fallen in the garden. The hollow was big and tall enough to hold Timo and the little bird.

As soon as he perceived the baby bird, Timo forgot about everything else, and ran after it until both of them arrived underneath the palm tree log. Timo was lying down flat on his belly inside that groove, and he was so fascinating observing that baby bird walking around the hollow. Based on his observations, the baby bird has tiny legs and its protruded belly was bigger than the rest of its body. He also noticed that the bird has a round little head and a tiny neck. Further, he observed and had noticed that its snout was yellowish, whereas its wholly body to appeared brown.

Timo was really having a lot of fun watching the bird walked back and forth underneath that hollow, which was surrounded by high and thick flowers. Nothing else mattered for Timo, but his new discovery.

His curiosity led him to forget about his family who could have missed him. He did not realize how long he and the baby bird had been underneath the log. He forgot about eating his favorite dishes ntere and mbisi and ntere and mikoso. Timo was just too excited and fascinating to observe that whole scenario. He eagerly held the baby bird for the first time since he was born.

Timo was not afraid to hold it. He got so involved playing with it down underneath the log that he forgot completely about coming out of it.

When the news broke that" **KAMINA**" was missing *–HE DISAPEARED*", all the neighbors became alert, and they spread the news everywhere. The search went on everywhere including in the neighbors' houses. Nobody knew where the child was. Timo could not be located anywhere. His mother was confused could not answer any questions from anyone, and right away she took the blame. I am the mother, and I should have known better how to keep an eye on a child. She was moving about with her arms spread out or upward, and some other time she was shaking her hands to express anxiety.

She certainly was afraid of her husband as well as her parents and uncle, Prince Mokwe, in the villages. She wondered what she could possibly say to them in order to justify such an awful action. Further, she was concerned of being called a negligent mother.

In addition, she knew how her husband adored the child; Denoza was in panic, and then she started to picture how the whole family would react concerning this situation. Her own justification was to start crying. She actually had turned the house upside down in the attempt to find Timo. Both servants stopped their routine activities, and went in search of Timo.

Finally, the husband had arrived and noticed that Timo was not coming to greet him as he always did. He opened the door, and shouted my prince! The father was expecting to see Timo running to greet him as usually, but it was not the case that evening. As soon as Timo's father had entered the house, he noticed however that his wife and both servants appeared puzzled. They stood unmovable without saying a word. Mr. Mikwaya noticed that there was a strange feeling in the air.

Further, he questioned what seemed to be wrong? Where is Timo? Denoza ran into the bed room, and lay in bed face down, and then started to cry. Mr. Mikwaya was frightened and all of a sudden dropped his bag on the table, quickly, and followed her in the bedroom. Anxiously, he asked Denoza, why are you crying. What seemed to be wrong here? Where is Timo? Denoza replied I do not know; we have been looking for Timo for the whole day, and we have no idea where he is.

What about the neighbors' houses, he asked anxiously. Everywhere we have been, and nobody seems to locate him, she replied. The father hearing this explanation, run out to start his own search. He went out in the garden to see whether or not he could have been by one of the fruit trees which had been his favorite hobby. Timo was not there unfortunately. The father asked the servants, "Did you verify whether or not the gate was open during the day?" The servants replied that we did double check and we had noticed that the gate was closed as usual. The father was really disturbed but where could the child be at this time? He wondered, hands on his waste!

All the neighbors who had gathered there to assist the family, decided to depart because there was nothing else they could have done at that point. All their efforts were exhausted. It was around 8:00 P.M.

Mr. Mikwaya, could not seat down and could not eat either. Actually, the whole situation had lost his appetite. He was determined to find his son, regardless. He ordered both servants to continue searching around the garden. Timo, on the other hand was so fascinating playing with the little bird underneath the hollow. He did not bulge to come out.

KAMINA WAS FOUND – COUGHT A BABY BIRD - KININI

After all the efforts were exhausted, Mikwaya and his two servants continued to stand outdoor looking around. All of a sudden, facing the palm tree log, the father noticed some movement, and there was flower trees 'movement. He ordered the servants, "Come on let us take a look under the log, it looked as though something is moving there."

Suddenly, Mr. Mikwaya, and both servants run to check, down there, and surely, they found the child sitting under the log. He was busy turning the baby bird back and forth. One the servant parted the grass then shouted, Timo is here. Mr. Mikwaya came running and his heart was beating so fast to see whether or not the child was fine. Suddenly, he pulled him out of the hollow. My prince, he shouted! Timo replied, yes, papa. He hugged him and kissed him. He asked him, what are you actually doing under this log? Timo eagerly raised showed his father the baby bird.

Papa, look what I found, a baby bird. He was excited telling his story to his father. His father was helpless, he could not reprimand him. Timo continued, I came here to play with my friend "Ki nini" that was the name Timo called the baby bird. Papa he is so funny, look, Timo let the baby bird on the ground, as he watched him walk, he was laughing with all his heart while his father and the servants were watching the scenario with a smile.

The father and all the servants were rejoicing, at last Timo was found. He is a little hero. He caught a little bird. They came in the house, the mother who was still crying in the bed room, suddenly, heard Timo's voice and came out quickly and hugged him and kissed him. Timo my son, she shouted! Where have you been all this time? Timo lifted the baby bird; all excited, and showed it to his mother. Look Mama, I have a friend called "KI NINI", he said, laughing. Mama, look at its protruded belly, he continued, mama look at his tiny but long feet. Timo was so satirical every time he mentioned a part of Ki NiNI's body. Finally, the neighbors heard Timo's voice, they also got excited. One of the neighbors notified the rest of his neighbors, saying to them, I heard that Timo was found. They could not help rushing to the Mikwaya's house to congratulate the parents.

KAMINA RELATIONSHIP WITH KININI- THE LITTLE BIRD

The bird was Timo's pet. He adored it with all his heart. Mr. Mikwaya ordered one of the servants to make a case for the little bird. It became a routine for Timo to run towards the cage everyday in order to feed and provide water to his so called friend "Kinini".

His parents and servants assisted Timo in providing, granulated grain such as corn, rice, gari (granulated cassava) other type of food. Kinini was growing daily because it was well fed, and Timo and his friends offered it a lot of love. The news spread out to his grandparents from both his mother's and his father' side as well as to his granduncle in their respective villages, they heard that Timo had discovered a baby bird on his own. Further they became aware that since the discovery of Kinini, Timo has become extremely happy.

Furthermore, his grandparents and granduncle heard also that Timo now has a cage made to shelter the little bird he had found. In addition, his grandparents were told that Timo has developed such an obsession about the bird.

They were also informed that as soon as Timo awaken in the morning, he runs to the cage to greet and sing a love song to Kinini, the title of the song was Luzolo (Love) -"KININI, KININI, Me Akuzol x 2 (means - Kinini , Kinini I love you dearly),"clapping his hands, then Kinini will be moving around the cage and sometimes it will be watching him quietly.

When Timo's little friends heard the news, they could not help running to his house in order to see the Mikwaya's bird out of curiosity. Timo was so courageous, and he repeatedly explained to everyone concerned, the circumstance under which he had actually met "Kinini, little bird. He used to tell his friends that "Kinini was actually a happy little bird who expressed its joy whenever I sing to him the love song which I dedicated to him." His friends started to get excited; they also wanted to learn the song, so that they too, could sing to Kinini as well whenever they came to visit it.

It was such a pleasure for Timo to teach them Kinini's love song. Timo knew that some of his friends' parents came from different villages and spoke different languages, and therefore, he took the time to explain the meaning of the song. He had told them, remember when I sing alone (singular), I must say "ME AKUZOL"-

I love you. When we sing in unison, we must say "BIS LAKUZOL" – we love you. Timo insisted also that they must clap hands when singing "KININI, KININI BIS LA KUZOL LA (X2). Timo was very influential, and his friends followed whatever he instructed them. Mikwaya was viewed as a hero among his little friends, in that neighborhood.

Timo and Ki Nini story amused everyone in his family, especially his grandparents and granduncle. Finally they too, came out with a great idea, and each grandparents and granduncle decided to offer Timo two baby pigeons, male and female; whereas his grandparents from his father's side offered him a little parrot instead. The servants brought five little birds altogether to "Far Away Town". The servants also assisted to build two more cages in the backyard, next to

Ki Nini's cage. One cage was designed for the four baby pigeons and another cage for the parrot. Timo was extremely happy and grateful to his grandparents for helping him to create a garden of birds behind his backyard. Timo's mind was so brilliant, told his parents to attach a tiny different cord around the pigeons' legs so that he could distinguish which pigeons are from his grandparents Mundu and which ones were from his granduncle, Prince Mokwe.

His parents thought it was an excellent idea. So, his mother attached a blue tiny thread on the pigeons' feet that came from his grandparents; Timo called them Koko Mundu and the ones that came from granduncle, were attached a green thread on their feet, and they were called Koko Mokwe.

Timo was so surprised in noticing that the parrot was actually repeating Ki Nini's love song afterwards. He named him the talking bird from grandparents Mikwaya.

The very first time that the parrot had actually sung was early in the morning, around 5:30 a.m. When Timo suddenly heard his love song was being sung, he woke up spontaneously, and wondered who in the world could be singing that song to Kinini besides from himself? He run to his parents' bedroom, Papa, mama, he called them eagerly, shouting; his father came running, what is the matter my prince? He asked. Timo asked his father, listen somebody is singing Kinini's love song in the backyard. Who is that person singing out there, Papa? His father replied, "Oh Timo go back to bed; that is the parrot repeating after you.

Papa, what did you say, the parrot? Timo asked? It is actually the bird which your grandfather Mikwaya and my mother had offered you, the father replied. Timo was so excited, Papa, can the bird sing? His father answered, yes, Timo, the parrot can repeat whatever you say; so you must be very careful about what you say.

Shortly after that, Timo continued eagerly, but Papa how is it that *KININI* never sings, during all this time that I have been signing to him? His father replied, Timo, when I come back from work tomorrow, I will have to teach you different kind of birds, so that you will understand their categories.

He continued, Kinini actually does not have the potential to sing, because it is not a parrot. That is why he cannot sing. However, the parrot is the only bird that has the ability to imitate everything that you said. Timo was really impressed to hear that a bird called parrot can actually sing his love song! Papa, if I would ask the parrot to sing along with me, can it do it?

It sounded so funny that his father had to laugh. However, Timo was so serious, and was actually staring at his father, and expecting to get a correct answer about the parrot. His father finally replied that, it was not possible," because you are a human being, and the parrot is a bird. Everyone must sing with his own kind."

CHAPTER IX

KAMINA FACED SCHOOL ADMISSIONS' ISSUES

All the kids of Timo's age were attending school, except Timo. The school system in a "Far Away Town" was just crazy as far as the constituents were concerned. The admission was based on a child's height instead of depending on his age. Denoza said to herself, it has been twice in a roll, Timo had been denied admission because of his height. Very soon the School administrator might be visiting every house to start measuring children's height once again in order to admit them in school.

How in the world would Timo be admitted in school this year, if he continues to maintain this tiny height? Denoza, started to cry. She blamed herself for accepting Timoli Mikwaya as a husband, a man who came from a modest background. She sometimes believed that her ancestors had punished her for marrying a man from a modest family, because she had a royal background. If her husband would have been from a royal family, probably her son Timo would have grown taller as her uncle Chief Mokwe and her father Chief Mundu. This was the manner in which Timo's mother justified the height of her son. She actually has been blaming herself at the inner level; however, she had never voiced it, until later on.

On one hand, Denoza was worried about her son. There was so much was going on in her mind. She wondered, if they do not let him attend school this coming year, what will the child be doing for the rest of his life? He will be staying around the house like a little dog? On the other hand, the child's father was very active. He always took the time to teach Timo at home. He was so bright and fast learner. The child enjoyed being around his father. His mother being a dress maker had tendency to wear a tape measure around her neck.

Timo hated to see the tape measure, because he knew that his mother used that tape measure as an object of criticism. One day, Timo's father was standing few steps away from him. Timoli saw her mother coming toward him with a tape measure around her neck. The tape measure was intended to take her customer's measurements for a dress she was planning to make. As soon as Timo's eyes saw that tape measure, he ran spontaneously towards his father, crying, no, no mama, please do not measure me today. All of a sudden, the child went to hold tied into his father's legs crying. His father asked him what the matter, Timo my prince is! Timo pointed at his mother's neck, and saying, look papa, that tape measure. Mama wants to measure me again crying, mama please don't measure me. His mother replied who is measuring you, Timo?

Mr. Mikwaya was surprised, did not know why the child was so frantic. Then he asked Denoza, what seems to be the problem with the tape measure? Denoza replied well you ask Timo himself. Mikwaya asked the child why you are crying. The child replied "The tape measure." He continued to ask him what about it? The child replied Mama always measures me, and she sings the song "*KAMINA, KAMINA ANALEY TO LA MAN* "every day when you go to work.

Then she tells me I want you to grow or else you will be a servant not a child. After telling his father his little misery, he went on crying. Mr. Mikwaya was disturbed to watch the child being so upset. Right away, he picked him up. He kissed him and continued telling him as usual. My little prince, remember always you are very handsome, very bright and very intelligent; you will go far away in life! You are so special, I love you very much. You understand me, he asked the child? The child was so happy and clapped his hands!

His father asked him to repeat. What your papa tell you? He repeated, papa always tells me, "I am so handsome, so bright and very intelligent. Therefore, I will go far away in life, because I am so special! His father replied, yes my boy! That is correct, you got it! Mr. Mikwaya was determined to offset all those negative statements regarding "Kamina which his wife had been addressing him repeatedly.

The father acted as a great psychologist to his son. He made it his business to have the child repeated on a regular basis all those positive statements about him in order to reverse the negativity. For the second time, Timoli and Denoza had another talk about the child; and it was on a Friday night while the child was sleeping. Mikwaya called his wife and pleaded with her to make him a promise that henceforth she will never again use that tape measure on the child? He said to her; see how fearful Timo appears to be?

Further, the father stressed in the fact that the tape measure has actually a negative effect on the child's brain. We do not want to lose the child, and we should really be very careful how we treat him. The mother had in reality developed a negative attitude towards the child; nevertheless, it was difficult to get her to change her mind. She replied with unkind tone of voice, well, if we do lose him, then that would be an indication that he was not meant to live, she concluded. The husband again begged her; please try to maintain a positive attitude towards the child from now on. I can assure you that Timo is a gifted child, and I truly believe that he will be successful by the grace of God, he added. Again, I confess that I trust in the power of the Living God that can alter anything.

CHAPITER X

KAMINA'S FATHER TRAVELLED TO ATTEND TEACHERS' SEMINARS OUT OF TOWN

Twice a year, it was mandatory for teachers to attend special school seminars out of town. The duration of the seminar varied from two to three days. Besides from her sewing activities, Denoza was known to be a multitasking woman. She also had a small Mikate (traditional donut) business. In addition, she has a small bakery. At first, Denoza used to make Mikate in a very limited quantity, and it was just for a social gathering. Her associates enjoyed eating her mikate they tasted delicious because of that special flavor. And therefore, all of them encouraged her to develop a small business from her wonderful talents.

In addition, she was advised and urged to appoint one of her servants to be in charge of selling mikate (donut) at the Mikate market. In fact, the selling activities ought to take place on a daily basis, and usually, very early in the morning when the construction workers, as well as all others, including merchants, vendors and buyers or customers began their daily activities. Mikate market was located not far from the Portuguese commercial busy area.

Portuguese's construction employees, the traders and all other customers that were coming and going from different villages were known as the potential mikate buyers. They were accustomed to eating mikate early in the morning for their breakfast. Therefore, Denoza was advised to prepare mikate on a timely manner, and instructed her salesman to arrive on time to the market.

Although, there had always been a variety of Mikate vendors, at the market, but since customers had tasted Denoza's mikate they were always in demand. Customers would be fighting over it on the first come and first serve basis, due to its Ginger flavor. Denoza was pleased with her first test. She actually designated a servant called Mabula to give it a try. Apparently it was very successful. However, during the time that Mr. Mikwaya would be away to attend the seminar, Denoza would wake up her son Timo at 4:30 am in order to keep her company in the kitchen while she would be making Mikate (donuts) during that time. The child would be moving up and down, apparently, falling asleep at the kitchen table.

The mother would be shouting at him, in the attempt to wake him up. Timo, I say stay awake! Get up and go put some cold water on your face! You have had enough sleep. You must keep me company, now. Keep talking to me about your bird Kinini so that you do not fall asleep! The child would start talking a little bit about how he met Ki Nini, but all of a sudden, he would begin waggling. Again, Denoza would shout at him, once more Timo, what did I say! Go put some cold water on your face. Stay awake and keep me company. He would give obedience. He would stand up and start shuffling, and then he would join her mother again. Shortly afterwards, the poor child would again begin to doze until at the end of mikate preparation session.

As previously indicated, Mabula was appointed as a mikate salesman. However, while Timo's father was away, Denoza found an excuse to get Timo out of the house during those days. She told her son, "Timo, now you will be going to the market with Mabula (the servant) you are going to start selling Mikate (donut) as well. At 7:00 a.m. Denoza would prepare a big size basket full of Mikate for the servant and one medium size basket full of Mikate for Timo (KAMINA) to carry to the market as well.

Denoza would giveTimo (Kamina) a Can or a container to keep the money for the sales of Mikate.

Apparently, Timo was so gifted, courageous, and so blessed that customers would be attracted towards him and buy his "Mikate quickly. Surprisingly, most of the time, Timo's Makati will be bought in a less than an hour. Because Denoza's mikate tasted delicious and completely different from every mikate found in that market. Timo was a well spoken child for his age. This child was proficient in the French language which happens to be the country national language. His father taught him both his native language as well as the French language.

KAMINA A SALESMAN AT MIKATE'S (Donut) MARKET

At the mikate market, the adult or the regular vendors, as soon as they started noticing how successful Timo was, they began to develop a high degree of jealousy against him. Timo's presence at the market began to disturb the regular vendors, and they started getting annoyed, every time Timo appeared at the "Mikate" market with his medium size basket full of Mikate.

The reason they hated him so much was due to the fact that he was a charismatic vendor. In fact, he attracted most of the customers. Customers were actually directed towards Timo, apparently for two main reasons: first, it was out of curiosity, to see how "KAMINA" acts. Then, second, because of the delicious taste of his mothers' Mikate.

Kamina could actually count his money very well, because his father had taught him Mathematics as well. However, an incident happened at the beginning of his salesman experience. Since customers became aware that Kamina's mother mikate were the best, and they were being sold out quickly, so as soon as Kamina would arrive, the crowd would actually rush and surround him. Everyone would have their money ready to pay for their part. Actually no customer wanted to miss the opportunity.

Therefore, three impatient customers, suddenly, rushed in through that crowd of customers that had surrounded Kamina, and suddenly, just laid their money on Kamina's laps at the same time. Then, they began claiming their mikate simultaneously. Kamina got somewhat confused in dealing with three people at the same time.

Each one was screaming his head off at him, "give me my mikate little boy, I just gave you my money!" Kamina was certainly frightened. All of a sudden, Mabula, the servant, who had been seating next to him, stood up quickly, and took the responsibility to clear that confusion. He gave each one his mikate based on the amount of money that was given. He also, reimbursed their change, and then calmly they departed. Certainly, Timo learned from that negative experience. He became aware that customers must actually hold on unto their money, and wait until their turn comes to be served.

As soon as his basket became empty, Timo would leave Mabula to continue selling his part. Then Timo would return home to give his mother the container full of money. His mother used to be overwhelmed with joy every time that Kamina would give her that container of money. She actually confirmed joyously that Kamina was indeed a successful salesman. He was capable in producing revenue. Apparently he must be a gifted child, she began to believe it.

As it was mentioned previously, at the "Mikate "market, customers always looked forward to seeing Kamina, and they would be rushing as soon as Kamina arrives with his basket full of tasty Mikate (donuts) in order to be "first come and first serve" before Kamina's donuts would run out. Unfortunately, customers were not aware that "Kamina" could only come to the market the days which his father was away for a meeting. Therefore the day that Kamina did not come to the market, customers would be standing, pacing up and down, waiting for Kamina. They would be holding their money in their hands.

Finally some customers would wind up buying mikate from other providers with regret. His competitors rejoiced exceedingly whenever Kamina did not show up at the market that day. They knew they will get all the customers. However whenever they perceived Kamina coming with his Basket full of Mikate, his competitors would be fuming inside. They would start whispering, "Here comes Kamina, today will be one of those bad business days for us, they would conclude. However, the customers had noticed one strange thing regarding this child, "Kamina".

Although he was smaller in height in comparison with all other vendors, he was however, the most powerful salesman. He knew how to discipline his customers. The minute any customer would attempt to touch one donut from the basket with his hand, Kamina would speak in a commanding voice, "excuse me, sir or madam, please take your hand off the Mikate Basket. You do not have to touch my mother's Mikate with your hands. My mother is strict, and she just does not allow this sort of mannerism. You must wait until I serve you." And, he would lift the big wooden spoon, saying, "Do you see this big spoon which my Mama had provided? Its function is to hold mikate for any customer who is buying it. Therefore, no one can touch mikate with hands."

However, Kamina would continue to instruct the people. He would say to them: "You as a customer, you are allowed to point out which one among the donuts you desire, and I will gladly get it with the spoon, and give it to you, as soon as you pay me your money. So, I beg you please never again touch the Basket with your hands!" He would say it sternly in order to make everyone aware.

Eventually, all the customers surrounding Kamina would actually pay attention. Everyone would therefore obey him; they would wait to be served by him. People around the market place would be so amazed to notice the power from this Small man who is speaking with such a powerful voice.

He spoke with authority, confidence, clearly, distinctively, and he stressed and articulated every word he pronounced. The employees and employers across the street could hear his voice clearly. At first they use to come out running to the market place to find out what is actually happening!

Kamina's mother used to always wish her husband to travel so that she would seize the opportunity to continue sending the child to the market in order to sell her mikate (donuts) and bring her quick money. Prior to starting school, Kamina had produced a lot of money for his mother. His mother used that money to open a bakery that was very successful as well. Denoza, Timo's mother was very compassionate. She used the money that was earned to send her cousins' children to school because three of her cousins married poor men who could not have afforded to send their children to school at all.

However, this period of time had to come to an end for Kamina. Timo Mikwaya was to start a different phase of his life. The course of things had changed rapidly for Timo.

KAMINA, EIGHT YEARS FACED SCHOOL ADMISSIONS' ISSUES

Two weeks later, the school administrator arrived in their house. He measured Timo who had just completed his eighth year, and yet his height was only one foot. As soon as the school administrator started to measure Timo, Denoza noticed that the man started to frown. Then, he mumbled, shaking his head, oh Madam, your son will have to wait until next year. I am sorry, the man said, Mrs. Mikwaya, your son cannot be admitted this year in school, because his height has disqualified him.

We go by the height of the child, madam, he added. The child is just too short to compete with the other children. If we do admit him at this height, this would mean that the teacher would have to devote most of his or her time just for him alone, and we feel that this would be inappropriate, not fair at all to the rest of the children, he concluded. Hearing this statement, Denoza became depressed, and then started to cry. She pleaded with the administrator to enroll him this year, by all means. She said to him, the year before the school denied him admission. Last year, he was denied admission as well. This year, please do not leave him behind again. Have mercy on my son, sir please, she pleaded. My son actually deserves a fair treatment. My son just happened to be a small man, a victim of circumstance. She continued to explain as the school administrator watched Denoza quietly. Evidently, he had noticed how upset the lady appeared to be, and suddenly, tears started streaming down her cheeks. Then, she resumed, sir, time is actually flying by quickly. You can view the child's appearance, sir. You can notice that Timo has started developing heavy buttocks and muscles, for the child of his age.

After having listened to the child's mother complaints, ultimately, the administrator asked the mother, "How old is Timo now?" She was so upset that she got it mixed up. She quickly replied that her son was seven years old now. At the same time, however, her husband was entering the house, and as soon as he had reached the threshold, he overheard the question and the answer given by Denoza. Suddenly, Mr. Mikwaya made a quick correction right then, saying, no, Timo actually had just turned eight- year-old last week.

Timo's father told the school administrator that "it is well that I find you here, so that I can seize this opportunity to speak with you about my son.

Denoza, my wife had reported to me that our son has been successively denied school admission by you, the school administrator. Unfortunately, I had always been absent every time you had come to measure Timo in the attempt to enroll him in school; You cannot imagine, sir, Mikwaya said, how painful it is to his mother, his father and especially to the child himself who feels eager to join his little friends in school. It actually breaks his heart to watch his friends walking to school, and he alone staying behind. The child has been asking us repeatedly how is it that his friends are attending school, and he is not. My wife and I feel awkward to answer this question. Actually, I just refuse to voice anything regarding his birth defect, because I want him to grow as a normal child, so that he can develop his self-esteem."

Mr. Kinkole sat there quietly, and the father's on continued, "the child has been suffering emotionally eventually, because he knows that he is eight year old currently, and he also sees all his friends, even those who are very younger than himself are attending school. The other day, Mr. Mikwaya continued, one of our servants saw Timo following his friends who were heading to school. Timo was walking along with them.

He had a note book in one hand and a pencil on the other hand. When he was asked, Timo where are you going? Timo replied, audaciously, I am going to school with my friends. Poor boy was not aware that prior to attending school, he had to be evaluated and admitted.

When the servant stopped him from following his friends, Timo grew very upset, and he ultimately, dropped himself on the ground; and then started to weep. The servant picked him up, and finally, brought him back home. The child was so quiet for that entire evening. He didn't have any appetite. When I had tried to cheer him up with one of our positive slogans which Timo knew and repeated on a regular basis, that day however, he could hardly pronounced the words. In spite of that distraction, Timo was determined to find out why he couldn't go along with his neighbors to school? It is actually very depressing to our son as well as to us, his parents, sir, because there was no relevant explanation or answer, Mr. Mikwaya added, scratching his ear.

The administrator began taking some note. Timo's father went on explaining, "I think we should make you aware, sir, that

Timo is a different kind of child, although he appeared to be a normal child." Mr. Kinkole asked him what do mean by that. Mr. Mikwaya replied, "The doctor had actually advised my wife and me that Timo will only be a small man. Further, he had said that he will not grow taller than one foot and half possibly." Hearing this statement, the Mr. Kinkole, the administrator was actually surprised and answered, "What kind of doctor would come out with that kind of nonsense, he exclaimed!

He continued, it appears as though, that individual probably is not a real doctor. He probably is just one of those individuals, who go around and just wear a white lab coats, and then hung a stethoscopes around the necks in the attempt to impress the public or just to showcase. In reality, those kind of individuals are those who usually get frantic when they are presented with serious medical cases; their brains and minds actually go blank or foggy! As a result, they utilize complicated scientific terminologies in attempt to confuse the patients and their families!

Mr. Kinkole continued, Mr. Mikwaya, I would truly advise you to, "Beware listening to some of those so called doctors' advice!" You should really take the time to shop around in order to find an excellent medical doctor, Mr. Kinkole concluded, while he was staring straight at the child's father face. He was at the same time, nodding his head, and rubbing his chin with his right hand.

The gentleman continued, Mr. Mikwaya, believe me, since I was born, I have never heard such a thing about a "little man or a child who would grow to reach only one foot and half tall!" That is just impossible, added the school administrator. How in the world, could that doctor predict a child's height? Is he God? If I were you, I would never believe in anything of that sort, you should put that picture out of your mind all together, he insisted.

I would bet, he continued, if you start feeding this child good nutrition, especially protein dishes such as, "NTERE", plus starch, corn and millet, also make sure the child eats Papaya, Mango, Banana and Orange. Do not forget to include Mwamb – A – Nguba (Peanut butter) on his bread. If you follow my advice, he said," you will actually notice that this child will grow taller than one foot and half; which that so called doctor has predicted. The gentleman crossed his hands over his head. He was actually nodding up and down, while he made comments regarding the child's height issue. I am sure about it, the man insisted.

Mr. Mikwaya and his wife experienced some kind of consolation hearing the word of encouragement from Mr. Kinkole. They thanked the gentleman for such a positive advice. However, Mikwaya insisted that his son be admitted to school that same year regardless. Denoza seized this opportunity to inquire about the following question, "My son is left-handed by the way, I wonder whether or not that would cause him a problem in school?

The school administrator replied "What! Is your son really left-handed? Oh, my gracious! Well, I would advise you to please make sure that you stop that bad habit. That is really peculiar, he insisted. Please help him as soon as possible. The best thing to do is to place a sock in his **left hand** in order to prevent him from using it. Watch him closely, and make sure that you change that pen or a pencil from left to his right hand as soon as you notice that peculiarity. In addition, do not be afraid to shout a little, Timo, hold that pen in your right hand, right now! The more you remind him from doing this, the sooner he will actually break that bad habit, said Mr. Kinkole.

Further, Timo's father revealed to the gentleman that he himself was a high school teacher. He explained to the school administrator that the child was already eight years old. He was requesting his understanding regarding this issue; the child was known as a small man. He could not therefore satisfy the measurement requirements. Therefore, based on these elements the child can be given a chance to attend school regardless to his small height. The school administrator turned to Denoza and told her, "Madam, please stop weeping, because your son Timo is now being admitted, and the school Director (Principal) will be made aware of this exception. I will make a special report to my superiors, Mr. Kinkole promised the couple. Denoza and Timoli felt very happy for the positive outcome of their meeting with the school administrator.

Finally, Mr. Mikwaya brought to the attention of the school administrator that, "this child, Timo, is very bright. I mean he is intelligent, and he is a fast learner as well. I, his father have been his first teacher, and I know my child is a gifted child; he spoke without any reservation. Further, Timo already knows how to read, to spell out words and to calculate.

He is fluent in French as well. If you so desire, sir, before you depart from my house, we will call Timo so that you can test him in whichever topic I have just mentioned or you can even start a conversation in French with him. I think it would be better if his mother and I would leave the living room for quite a while, and leave both of you alone. Please be free to make your own evaluation, Timoli said to the gentleman.

The school administrator was just curious to find out the truth of every word Mr. Mikwaya had spoken regarding his son's aptitude. He was very anxious to test Timo right then. So, Timo was called in the living room, and left his friends outdoor. He was introduced to the school administrator, Mr. Kinkole.

Immediately, the gentleman started a conversation in French with Timo. "Bonjour" Timo, he said, Timo replied in French, "bonjour Monsieur Kinkole "(Hello Mr. Kinkole). At this point, Mr. Kinkole took interest to assess the child further. He asked him "what is your name?" (Comment t-appelles-tu?) – The child replied, "je m'appelle Timo Mikwaya mais ma mère aime m'appeler Kamina des fois"(my name is Timo Mikwaya, but my mother called me "KAMINA" sometimes.

Mr. Kinkole asked him, «pourquoi t-appelle-elle Kamina des fois? (Why does she call you Kamina sometimes?)" At this point, Timo turned his head from left to right, prior to replying, and finally he answered, "Well, because of my special height, I believe (Je crois à cause de ma taille speciale).

Mr. Kinkole continued assessing Timo, "Timo can you write your name on this piece of paper?" The child answered, yes I can. Then he spelled out his name so quickly. Mr. Kinkole asked Timo spontaneously, three oranges plus five oranges how many oranges that amount to? The child answered equal to eight oranges. Mr. Kinkole called his father and mother finally, to join them in the living room. They came back quickly, and were anxious to hear the results of Mr. Kinkole's assessments. Apparently, he was so excited, and he said to Timo's parents: "the child is certainly so bright. He speaks clearly, and also stressed in every word he pronounced. He could add, subtract very fast. In addition, Timo was able to recite the multiplication table without any hesitation. Mr. Mikwaya, your son is a genius! I marvel observing him. The child's father replied that I actually have been teaching him since he was three years old.

Currently, he is eight years old, so that is another fact that any individual should really consider to admit my son in school this year. The school administrator evidently regretted his previous and poor judgment concerning the child. He felt guilty for not admitting the poor child sooner, due to his height. The school administrator was actually a narrow minded person. He had never heard or read anything regarding "midgets."

Further the school administrator called Timo again, and asked him, Timo would you like to start school next month? The child's eyes were wide open, and he jumped, then clapped his hands above his head, replying with joy, "YES, yes, yes! I do want to go to school." The child was overwhelmed with joy. Timo was not a shy child; Right in front of the gentleman and his parents Timo went on naming his friends, saying, "I will start going to school with my friends, Nona, Adolfo, Muku Ngago and Kisele.

The school administrator and the child's parents were all rejoicing, exceedingly to witness the child's enthusiasm and willingness to begin school soon. Denoza had tears of joy for the first time, however, a little sad knowing that Timo was not aware that his little friends were already in an advanced class and that they would never be in the same class ever. Probably his next question around the school would be." Why can't I be in the same class with my friends?" It is ashamed, Timo will be starting Kindergarten at the age of eight year old, unnecessarily, his mother would say to herself.

At last, things are about to change for Timo's life. His misery in regard to denial of school admission will apparently be dissipated. Certainly, one day, he will be sadly recalling the consecutive events of his childhood; such as how he used to remain lonely behind. Further, how devastated he felt to watch other kids of his ages walking along the friends in a group of five or six to school, joking and giggling on their way to school.

Eventually, the majority of things would become nothing but historical in the near future as well for Timo. Furthermore, Timowould not forget to recall how his mother used to become sympathetic and weep to watch her son turning around the garden alone with a piece of paper and a pencil in his hand. Sometimes Timo would be seen, talking to the flowers. And the other time, he will be seen, sitting under a fruit tree; and then drawing a shape of the fruit.

Sometime however, Timo would lay flat on his belly and would be lifting his head up and down in order to observe the fruit and then draw it on the paper. His favorites drawing consisted of either an orange, or a banana or a palm nut or a palm branch with leaves attached to it. At the other time, Timo would also be seen

lying on his back facing the sky, just resting and humming "Kamina song."Kamina's school acceptance was such a relief to his family and especially to himself.

Ultimately, Timo will be starting school in a couple of months; he will be joining with his friends to school. What a joy to his parents, even though he would begin from Kindergarten; and he also will be the older kid in his class. It was a consolation to his parents to know that at least Timo could already read and write, and do mathematics. Besides, Timo had a very clear speech. He knew how to articulate his words when he spoke. Apparently he took after his father.

CHAPTER XI

KAMINA'S SCHOOL EXPERIENCE FROM KINDERGATEN TO HIGH SCHOOL

The first teacher Timo had was female, she was called Ma Sala. Surprisingly, the teacher was able to notice something unusual about the child called Timo. He had a pierced look, and he had the ability to immediately recognize any picture drawn on the board. Besides, he was always busy helping his classmates. The teacher, Ma Sala took a deep interest in observing Timo, because he was very remarkable. After one month, Mrs. Ma Sala wrote a special report about the child called "Timo Mikwaya" also known as Kamina. The report to the school Director read as follow:

Dear Director Tala-Tala,

I am writing to inform you that among the twenty students that are enrolled in my class, I am noticing something which I have never noticed since I have been teaching here. The child Timo Mikwaya appeared to be so special. He can read, write, and draw extremely well for a child who is in this level.

And besides, he is busy helping his classmates. As I watched him, I often noticed a group of children gathered around him; they all asking him questions, and he answers them correctly too. The only problem is that he is left-handed, but he is learning to write sometimes with his right hand. His intelligence exceeds this class level. I would recommend that the child be placed in an advanced class. It would be indeed a waste of his time and not fair to other kids who need to proceed slowly. Signed - Ms. Ma Sala

The Director evaluated the child and found him indeed to be a gifted child. So the school decided to place Timo in an advanced class. Timo was now in the First grade. Two months later, the teacher of the First grade, Mr. Mupasa noticed how bright the child appeared to be. He could write, read, calculate and draw very well. His mind and brain were so alert. What was so amazing and impressive to the teacher was to notice the manner in which the child could articulate in his speech. Mr. Mupasa was so curious at first. And then, he would call him privately and speak with him alone. He was so impressed to notice the intelligence in this child. Then he decided to make further assessment by asking him few questions.

The first question was "what is your father's name? The child answered my father's name is Timoli Mikwaya. Then he was asked again what about your mother's? Timo replied that his mother's name was "Denoza Mundu Mikwaya." Mr. Mupasa told him perfect Timo, rubbing his head.

Then, again the teacher had asked Timo, "Do you know how to spell out the names of your parents, father and mother?"The child eagerly replied, yes, I do. Timo told Mr. Mupasa, teacher, I also know how to spell out my own names. Mr. Mupasa was getting a kick out of this child. Mr. Mupasa told him, Timo, very well. Show me how do you spell your father's and your mother's names?" , Mr. Mupasa gave him a piece of paper, then right away, Timo wrote his father's name –

T I M O L I M I K W A Y A and my mother's name is **D E N O Z A M U N D U** MIKWAYA.

Mr. Mupasa asked Timo – now draw the shape of an Orange. Timo drew a shape of orange and inserted a stem on top of the shape. When he was asked spitefully to explain the reason why he had added the stem on the top of the orange format, the child answer, was well, "Well you see, this is actually a slender part that holds the orange on the branch while it is growing. He then elaborated the explanation in his own childish words. adding and, it is like a hand you see that holds a mother's hand he concluded. The teacher was shocked to hear such a precise explanation from that child.

Mr. Mupasa asked Timo, "Where did you learn how to read and write so beautifully like this? The child replied, "My father teaches me every day when he comes from work. Further, he said my father always calls me a smart boy, a very bright boy, and my little prince. Timo answered giggling. Based on this assessment, Mr. Mupasa wrote also a report to the Director stating:

Dear Director Mesa,

Two months ago, a child was placed in my class, called Timo Mikwaya also known as KAMINA due to his aptitude. This child is extremely intelligent. I believe that he really should be placed in an advanced class.

He knows *more than every student in my class. He is so gifted, and I feel that there is no need to waste his time. He should really be learning more advanced lessons. I personally made an assessment, and found out that Timo deserves to be in the next level. I can prove how the child performed during the assessment session, if you so desire. As far I am concerned, the only problem this child has is the fact that he is a left-handed however he can write very fast in spite of his disability.*

The Director could not doubt Mr. Mupasa's report, because Ms. Ma Sala had previously made the same recommendations. Timo was placed in the second grade immediately. The child was moved successively within the same year, from Kindergarten to the First grade, and from the First grade to the Second grade.

In the Second grade, his new teacher was called Miss Lakele. The director advised Ms. Lakele to observe this child, "Timo Mikwaya" very carefully and to report his progress immediately. Timo was not shy. Every child was conversing with him. Mr. Lakele gave Timo a close attention. She noticed that the child could read and write his name well.

Further, he loved Mathematics, and he is very capable to add and subtract with no problem. Mr. Lakele was impressed to notice the manner in which the child articulates the words in his speech. He was well spoken. Finally, the teacher asked Timo, "who taught you how to read, to write, and to draw so beautifully like this? Timo replied my father is my teacher at home too.

His is always teaching me and I love to learn new things, he replied eagerly. Ms. Lakele noticed that every time she wrote a Mathematics exercise on the board, Timo was able to add and subtract with accuracy, faster than any other student. Timo has a very good hand writings, although he was left-handed. Ms. Lakele was impressed with these observations. Ms. Lakele made a comment, and concluded that this child was indeed gifted.

She waited until he completed the second grade and told the Director that this child should be actually placed even in the fourth grade his intelligence way above average. He scored always higher than any other kid in class. Ms. Lakele also added that Timo's classmates cannot keep up with him. Apparently, they feel intimidated by his aptitude.

The school year ended, Timo has gone from Kindergarten to second grade in one year.

He was eight year old, and still appeared short for his age. When his parents, Denoza and Timoli received his report from school, they were overwhelmed with joy. At first, the child did not know that it was all about him as he observed his parents rejoicing. Suddenly, the father came and picked him up and hugged him, and then his mother came afterwards, hugged him while he was still in his father hands. Ultimately, they decided to explain to the child. Timo, said Mr. Timoli, you are doing very well in school. Remember you are an intelligent Boy! My Prince, and you will go far away in life, he hugged him again and again. The child was so accustomed with all the positive statements from his father, and he began to giggle, Papa I know you always say those things to me, and I told my teacher too about it, laughter!

So, the child returned to school and started the fourth grade. The fourth grade teacher's name was Ms. Bibuana. Timo was nine years old but appeared to be the shortest in his class. Timo was so bright in school even though he did not attend the third grade. Timo was being watched carefully, because every teacher was aware of this child's ability to learn. He spoke clearly, and articulated in every word he said.

He wrote clearly, and he knew his multiplication table by heart. When his teacher asked him where did he learn how to recite the multiplication table? He replied explicitly, "I learned it from my father, and he is my teacher at home. My father views me always as a very smart boy. He tells me often that "Timo you will go very far in life," Timo used to giggle whenever he repeated his father's slogan to his teachers.

The teacher began challenging Timo as soon as he came in his class. In order to evaluate his school aptitude in the fourth grade, the teacher had modified his teaching methodology for awhile. Each morning, he would start with a prayer, and therefore, the teacher also decided to select two students per day to step up and pray. One child would begin the prayer and the other would close the prayer session. The majority of the students were afraid to assume that responsibility. They were inexperienced to utter any prayer, but Timo was always eager and courageous to pray every time he was selected. The most amazing thing was to hear that child pray.

He knew how to start his prayer with "Heavenly Father." He prayed for himself first of all, and then he would pray for his parents. Subsequently, he would pray for his teacher Ms. Bibuana; and finally he would also say, "God please help everyone in this class. Help everyone in the hospital. Help everybody in this country and those in the entire world. This is how his father trained him to pray, and he did it systematically.

Ms. Bibuana once called Timo privately and questioned him about his parents. He told her their names. Before the teacher had the chance to ask him what kind of job does your father do? The child on his own volition continued, my father is a teacher, but he teaches the big people only. However, every evening, he teaches me at home, how to read and write plus math. In addition, he teaches me how to pray, at the dinner table, as well as before going to bed. My father tells me that I am a very intelligent boy, and that I will go very far in life, Timo giggled.

Ms. Bibuana was so thrilled to hear all these things from a nine year- old. She knew that this child was indeed gifted. She also noticed that every question that was asked in class,

Timo would always raise his hand in the attempt to answer, whereas other students would appear bashful. Most of the time, his answers would be correct or close to that. Ms. Bibuana also thought it was necessary to notify the school Director (Principal) about this student. The Director was pleased to see that even Ms. Bibuana, the teacher of the fourth grade had noticed something on her own without previously being told.

The Director spoke with Ms. Bibuana, and he confirmed that "all your predecessors had noticed something unusual about the child called "Timo Mikwaya, known also, as KAMINA." Ms. Bibuana told the Director that "I would like to try something new for further evaluation of Timo." I will select about five bright students in my class, and I will include Timo as well. I actually would like to test their spelling and a math aptitude, and this will be actually to evaluate Timo's intelligence which would help us to determine whether or not we can make some other recommendations about this child. The teacher actually received the Principal's approval and then tested all the six students. Timo scored higher than the five other students.

In fact, he finished the test way before his classmates. Ms. Bibuana could not actually wait until the end of the class period in order to report that exciting outcome to the Director. She immediately brought all the six tests results, and showed them to the Director. When he saw Timo Mikwaya's test and the grade, he really confirmed that indeed this child is a very gifted boy. He should not waste his time in the fourth grade any longer. He then transferred Timo to the fifth grade during the same school year. Timo was the only left-handed child in the entire school.

Timo stayed in the fifth grade, then from that time on he continued moving the rest of his classes gradually until he graded from the elementary school. During his entire elementary school years, Timo had always been busy helping his classmates with their school challenges. His parents were always being invited to school in order to attend school parties given in the honor of those elementary students who exhibited a higher degree of intelligence. Few months later Mr. Mikwaya and his wife decided to share Timo's new life with his grandparents and granduncle.

Ultimately, the grandparents also learned that heir great grandson had been admitted in school, and that he was brilliant in every subject. That letter actually had brought a lot of joy to Denoza's family as well to Timoli Mikwaya's family. Their misery turned into joy. They spread the good news again through the entire villages where the people had previously experienced a lot of concern regarding Timo's known miseries both his height, as well as his denial of school admission in the past few , and consecutive years. Everyone had to share that piece of information. "Did you hear that Chief Mundu's great grandson, Denoze's son is currently attending school and that everyone teacher is speaking about his high degree of intelligence, they are saying that he is a Genius? Positive people began to shout, "Oh, God knows how to change things around, from a negative situation to a positive situation!" At this point, the critics who had formed the habit to poke fun at Denoza were unable to continue doing so.

Ultimately, all of those people began realizing that Timo's height problem was a punishment neither from God nor from Denoza's ancestors.

Timo Mikwaya, ultimately, completed his elementary school as an excellent student, and was admitted in a very reputable High School in Kinshasa. He was going from glory to glory. At first, people around his school were so curious to watch him walk and talk, because they were not accustomed to seeing a man of such a small height. Eventually, people got use to that view afterwards. As soon as he began High School, Timo's talents could not be hidden. All his teachers started to speak highly about him in that new location. Further, his classmates, noticing his intelligence, they too started seeking for help in their home work. Timo has always been compassionate, and began tutoring his classmates who used to request his help.

Timo was exceptionally known for his intelligence and his height. Mr. and Mrs. Mikwaya have always been happy to see their child's school's report card. In every class he attended, Timo had the highest grade. Almost all of his teachers assigned him a special role to play in class, and he played it satisfactorily. Timo went from glory to glory moving from one class after another all through High School. At this time, Timo exceeded the predicted height. People actually began to notice a big difference from his height.

He had actually grown from one foot to two feet and half. That change in height has actually occurred because of his father's faith. He prayed a lot about this issue. He had just refused to believe that Timo had to stop growing at the height of one foot and half.

CHAPTER XII

KAMINA TRAVELLED TO BELGIUM TO PURSUE HIGHER EDUCATION

The school awarded him a scholarship to start the University education in Belgium. Prior to his departure to Belgium, his grandparents, Chief Mundu, his wife Kibo and grand uncle, Prince Mokwe along with his wife Mikoke all of them decided to go to "Far Away Town" in order to bid Timo goodbye. Further, they would also seize that opportunity to discuss with Timo's parents whether or not it was a good idea to let Timo travel to Europe without being accompanied by any other Congolese student or a guardian. They were somewhat concerned about his height and the people's injustice around the world.

The grandparents appeared frightened, thinking that they might not see him again. They started to imagine all kinds of negative things, but Timo was so confident. He assured them with conviction, grandparents and granduncle, as well as their wives that, he shall be back; they need not to worry. He believed that everything would go just smoothly.

Mr. Timoli Mikwaya, spoke with confidence to his in - laws, saying: "My wife Denoza and I believe in God's will and in God's decision. I am glad to see that you love Timo as much as we love him. We all are going to miss him for the time that he will be away. The reason he is not traveling in a group of Congolese students is due to the fact that Timo had passed the exam that his School gave to twenty five students in the attempt to select an appropriate candidate, and eventually the one who would score higher than the rest of the students.

Timo's score was higher than his classmates, and he was awarded the scholarship. Apparently there was only one scholarship available, therefore he must travel alone because the accommodation has been done for him alone.

We sincerely believe that Timo is a gifted child, and what God wants to do with Timo, we as his parents must not interfere except to continue praying for him, said his father.

FAMILY GATHERING PRIOR TO DEPARTURE TO BELGIUM

Prior to the day of his departure, there was a dinner given in the honor of Timo, that evening. All the neighbors and Timo's friends were invited. All the servants worked harmoniously well together; those who had accompanied Chief Mundu as well as those who came with Prince Mokwe. They were six servants altogether including those who had been living with Timo's parents. The Cooks made sure to include Timo's favorite dishes, ntere and mbisi (pumpkin seed with fish) as well as ntere and mikoso (pumpkin seed with Shrimps or baby shrimps). The Pastor and his wife were invited as well. Prior to serving dinner, the Pastor read one verse of the Scripture, and then he conducted a prayer in order to bless the food. People ate and drank well.

Finally, to close the evening, the Pastor again spoke, "we now going to bid goodbye to Timo.

May God be with you and bless you Timo on your journey, and give you his wisdom in everything you will be doing in the future until we meet once again." Timo was deeply touched. He stood up and thanked all of the guests for honoring him that evening. Timo said: "To my Pastor and his wife, to my parents, to my grandparents and to my granduncle, Prince Mokwe and his wife, as well as to all my friends, I know that it is God who has selected me among my classmates, and it is God also who is sending me abroad. I am actually aware that where I am going, I do not know anyone so to speak. I can understand the fearful spirit that is coming from my grandparents in regard to H however, I can confirm that I do know one Great Being, and that Being is" God!" Timo concluded. Hearing Timo's statement, the Pastor stood up eagerly, and lifted the Bible up in his right hand, and shouted, "There we go people! God, the Almighty is really our Friend everywhere we go. He is here, He is there and He is everywhere! He added joyously.. Then suddenly everyone else stood up spontaneously, and applauded. It was a happy ending, and everyone bade Timo goodbye.

So, the next day, Timo was escorted to the airport in order to catch his 9:00 p.m. flight to Brussels.

Timo was always a well dressed boy. Timo's parents and his grandparents, as well as his granduncle, Prince Mokwe had formed the habit of offering him different types of gifts including monetary.

On the day which Timo was traveling, his parents made sure to pack nothing but his best suits, his traditional shirts and sport jacket (demi-dakar), and also his best shoes. His grandparents and granduncle each of them had sold one cow and the money received was given to Timo as his pocket money. Mr. Timoli Mikwaya, his father, had a very talented tailor who always made his best suits as well as his son's Timo's suits. He made both western and traditional outfits, Congolese fine style. The day Timo was traveling he was dressed up in his favorite blue color suit. The tailor had exemplified his expertise in making Timo's suits and jackets. He appeared as sharp as a little prince would appear.

At the airport, the crowd was gathered around Timo. This scenario attracted everyone's attention. One of the Sabena Airlines agents asked people around her, "Who is that gentleman surrounded by all those people? One of the flight attendants replied, that is the famous guy, called "Kamina".

Some agents had never seen a midget before. Therefore, they took the opportunity to run towards the crowd in order to take a close look of Kamina. One of them was excited, and then she exclaimed in French, "dit donc, c'est un petit nain (oh, my God, he is a midget!). He is traveling, but where is he travelling to? All the agents were excited to see Timo for the first time. Another agent commented, "but he is really handsome, too bad that he is too short, and he sounds with such a deep beautiful voice for such a small person," she said.

Half an hour prior to departure, Sabena airlines agent made an announcement: "will the passenger "Timo Mikwaya come to the information counter please! " Every family member got excited hearing his name called through the loud speaker. Therefore, they began saying to each other, "oh Timo is being called", and then, suddenly, Timo, his father and his mother immediately ran to the counter. Timo's parents told the agent, Timo is our son. This is his very first trip to Europe. Do you think that he is going to be OK? The agent replied eagerly with a smile, "Surely Madam, he is going to be perfectly fine.

Do not worry about that. That is our expertise actually. We make sure that all our passengers are well taken care of." Another agent turned towards Timo, and said, "Timo can I have your passport please?" Immediately, he opened his tote bag which was hanging on his left shoulder, and took out his passport. He glanced at it first, and then gave it to the agent. The agent verified his passport quickly, and at the same time checked his luggage. He gave him his boarding pass, and advised him to be seated, and wait for fifteen minutes until further instructions are announced.

Fifteen minutes later, the announcement was made for the passengers to Brussels to start boarding. Timo immediately approached his friends and family. He shook hands, and then run towards his folks. Chief Mundu, his grandfather, lifted him by his chest and hugged him. Finally, he whispered, "Remember to write and let us know how things are going over there.

Should people mistreat or undermine you, just inform us, and we will do everything in our power to send you money so that you can buy a return ticket home immediately. Do you hear what I have just said, prince?"

He looked straight into his eyes, and Timo smiled at that. He shook his head and assured him that I am pretty sure things will go well, grandpa. He replied, "We will continue to trust in God as you do," grandpa added.

Subsequently, Prince Mokwe, who was his granduncle lifted him by his chest as well, and hugged him; he whispered, saying "Remember, Timo, you are my heir. I will start telling your mother everything she would have to transmit to you, in case I am no longer alive by the time you will come back from abroad." Timo was so courageous, and changed that sad thinking. He said, "granduncle Mokwe, of course we shall see each other again, by the grace of God. Years go by so fast do not forget that. I will make sure to write to you and tell you about my experience abroad. Prince Mokwe was so delighted to notice Timo's courage. Then, finally, came his loving father, Timoli Mikwaya lifted him by his chest also, and hugged him and kissed him, rubbing his head.

While he was being held by his father, Denoza his mother hugged and kissed him as well. Both of his parents told him, Timo our love, go in peace with God.

We know things are going to be the way God wants them to be. They also whispered in his ear, "Remember do not break your prayer routine, before and after bed time. Make sure you read a verse of Scripture, and sing to God. I did pack your lyrics book and the Bible as well, said his mother.

His father rushed to remind him, remember our slogan son, always, "if God can part the ocean, God can also bridge the gap!" This is the statement that had helped me to marry Denoza, the Chief's daughter, your beloved mother. Timo looked at her with a smile. His father stated, "Asked her how much she actually hated me when I was making an attempt to propose to her, he added, smiling. Timo turned to her mother, and Denoza, giggled, waggling her head, and ultimately, she confirmed the statement. Denoza, held Timo by his right shoulder and whispered, "Timo your father really has faith in God. I surely believe in the Power of the Living God currently.

Timo replied, Mama, I rejoice to hear you talked positively about spiritual matters, please continue to have that faith in the future until we meet again, he told her.

His mother continued, Timo, your father was actually right when he repeatedly said to you, "you will go far away", and see now, it has manifested. Like a dream you are now going far away, she added. Timo replied, yes, Papa is a positive man. I used to laugh about that statement sometimes, but that statement actually has helped me to build confidence. It is indeed meaningful and powerful as well. His mother agreed with Timo.

Suddenly his mother said, "Remember you are going miles away, we will love to read your correspondence on a regular basis. You actually should keep us abreast of how actually things are going over there in terms of your education. By the way, she continued, I would like to inform you prior to departure that your school had requested that we send enough money so that they can actually buy you good all the necessary outerwear for winter. Therefore we had done that.

We trust that they will buy good qualities (coat, boots, scarf, gloves and a hat) and bring them to the airport where you will be picked up.

Few minutes later, the flight attendant advised Timo, "O.K. Mr. Mikwaya, hold your boarding pass in your hand, and come on to the gate. It is a boarding time, she said to him." After waving to all of his friends and family, Timo stood up on the line behind a very tall man with his boarding pass in his hand. And then, the agent, torn one part and gave him the other part. She did it with a very big smile. So, the flight attendant escorted him to his seat. She knew that that trip was the very first one for Timo, and therefore they had made sure to give him an enjoyable journey.

However the pilots and the crew realized that the time was still early to take off. The commander was kind enough to allow the flight attendant in charge of Timo, to walk him out of the plane so that Timo could have another opportunity to wave once more at his family, and friends, who were still gathered outside, at seating area. As soon as they arrived at the threshold of the gate, the crowd suddenly stood up facing Timo, and began cheering, chanting and waving, goodbye, Timo! – Goodbye Timo! – Timo we love, we love you!

Shortly after waving back at them, he finally was escorted inside the plane; where he was assigned an aisle seat. The Pilots and his entire crew were so happy to be able to carry such a famous little guy on board. The atmosphere was just pleasant and joyous. Most of the passengers were so eager and curious to observe Timo, who was travelling for the very first time abroad. Everyone could feel the excitement in the air.

TIMO'S EXPERIENCE AT THE BELGIUM'S AIRPORT

When he arrived in Brussels, he noticed everyone was so interested in his height. People turning behind to watch him walk. He was accustomed to being an object of curiosity, but he was confident. He knew that he was handsome lad, he was proficient in French, he also knew that he was intelligent and he was going to make it. Timo kept a positive attitude and was fearless.

At the airport, the people who were assigned to pick him up, and bring him to the University campus could not spot him right away.

He was lost in the crowd among the passengers. One of them spotted him as he neared the exit. He said to his colleague, I think I see him coming. He is between those tall men, he exclaimed! He has on a blue suit and a white shirt. He is holding a navy blue bag. Oh, exclaimed one of the colleagues, Is he a midget? Oh I was not aware of this fact, neither was I, the other person added.

Another gentleman said, "let us stand right at the exit where he can see us, and hold the sign with his name clearly, not too high because he is a small man. At first, he did not notice the sign right away, and then one of the gentlemen called his name, Timo but still did not pay attention because there was so much noise. Another gentleman yelled, Timo Mikwaya, Kamina, all of a sudden, he looked towards the sign, quickly he approached them. They greeted him happily, but the big problem was the coat which they had actually bought him was way too big for his size. In addition, Timo noticed that it was not the high quality of material that Timo's family would have selected for prince, Timo Mikwaya. Why did this dilemma occur?

Congo having a hot climate, does not sell any outwear or winter equipment. When the money was sent to the people in charge, in order to buy Timo a high quality coat in Belgium, there had been a communication gap.

Apparently those in the Congo, who were assigned to arrange Timo's school matter with their correspondents in Belgium actually failed to establish a clear communication about Timo's physical information, such as reporting his height as well as his weight. All these important elements were in fact forgotten to mention. It was assumed however that the preliminary information that was previously transmitted was correct. Apparently only partial information had been transmitted, thereby omitting the crucial information about Timo. They should have evidently stressed on the fact that Timo was actually a *Small Man,* and that it was imperative to buy him a *small size outwear* and *size four shoes.* In fact, the problem originated from the picture that was previously forwarded to Brussels. Instead of forwarding a full length picture, they had sent rather a passport photo showing only his beautiful face and his beautiful smile.

Further, the other information was more about his family background. They elaborated more about the fact that his grandma was a princess from one of the ancient African Kingdoms, and his father was a School teacher who measured six feet two tall. Therefore, due to the fact that Timo's height and weight were never specified, those gentlemen who were meeting him at the airport, in Brussels had assumed that Timo must have been six feet tall as well. Therefore they bought him a *decent coat*, but *size eighteen instead of buying him a size five.* They also bought him a *decent pair of boot size fourteen instead of size four*. Then, when they actually had arrived at the airport, looking at a small man coming out of the gate, both gentlemen almost fainted as they looked at each other, they were puzzled. They knew that they were facing a serious problem. The car was parked about one block away from the airport. The weather was about thirty two degree Fahrenheit.

Timo Mikwaya has a medium size luggage and his tote bag. Now, the gentlemen realized that he is too small, and the coat is too big and also too long for his height. They had no money available on hand to even think about providing him an appropriate size coat and boots at that time.

In addition, it was too cold for a person coming from a hot weather to face that degree of cold also. The two gentlemen wondered which approach to take. The only wise decision was to wrap Timo in that big coat as a baby, and to carry him horizontally, and then bring him into the car. One of them went to bring the car closer to the exit in order to make it easy for transporting him. First of all, they took his luggage and tote bag, and placed them in the trunk.

Further, both gentlemen explained to him the situation, so they lifted Timo, well wrapped in that big coat in order to prevent him catching cold, and then he was placed in the car, where he was seated in the back seat. Then they drove him to the University campus.

Finally, he was escorted to the University campus where he was shown his room, and was given all the necessary information needed to familiarize him with the environment. The following day, the gentlemen in charge decided to buy him a petit size navy blue coat and size four boots with Timo's allowance money.

The coat and the boots were suitable to his size, and he was very happy with them because navy blue happened to be his favorite color.

Prior to starting the academic year, the University decided to test Timo in order to make an assessment of his school aptitude. The Dean of the Political Science Faculty disdained Timo at first view. He did not believe that Timo Mikwaya (Kamina) would be able to succeed. He wondered why the School in the Congo couldn't send a tall student instead. Because of his doubt and fear, the Dean ordered the staff to test Timo in French literature and in Mathematics. Timo was called and advised to take all these tests prior to registering. The Dean decided that if Timo does not pass both tests he would have to send him back to the Congo, and he would ultimately be replaced by another qualified student, implying of course to a medium height or a taller student.

Timo was confident that he was going to pass, and did not mind to take both tests the next day. When he was given the literature test, Timo noticed that it was based on his favorite French writer, Molière. He scored higher than the Dean had expected.

It was the same for his mathematic test, he scored even higher than everyone had expected. Based on his scores, Timo was allowed to register, right away.

The faculty talked about Timo, he is a small man with a very extensive brain and high intelligence. He was loved by his professors and his fellow students, because he was always available and willing to assist those students who were facing difficulties in Mathematics, Calculus and Accounting, Mikwaya was always asked how is it that he was able to comprehend all these hard courses. His answers had always been "I believe that it is just a gift from God. Everyone has his or her own natural gift. In respect to my gift, I would say that my gift has to be my brain. I. sincerely believe that this gift was given to me in order to compensate with my small height". Timo would shrug afterward, and he always replied with a little smile in order to conclude his statement. Additionally, he would say, I truly believe that everyone was given a special gift, which is different from everyone else. I guess, this could be to prevent world-weariness. Basically, human beings like varieties, don't them? That is why people have different cultures.

CHAPTER XIII

TIMO'S ASSOCIATION WITH FELLOW STUDENTS – TUTORING SESSION

Because of his little height, during the tutoring session, a comfortable chair was always provided for Timo to stand on while he was writing on the board to explain the course to his fellow students. Everyone in that room felt obligated to respect him, and he would sense it too. On Friday, it was almost at the end the session when one of the students had asked him an informal question, "Mr. Mikwaya, how do people view you?" Timo stressed more on the word Respect or LUZITU to answer this question, and gave more examples regarding his own life. He said people often have discrimination concerning the word "LUZITU"or Respect. They do not always start treating somebody with LUZITU (respect) unless they know the social status of that individual, or they are just impressed by the appearance of that particular individual. Let us take for example myself, based on my appearance I actually undergo plenty of negative remarks. Negative nick names do not always come from strangers, sometimes they could come from your own closer association or relatives.

Timo went on explaining few things about his personal life, "I do not know whether or not you have heard my other nick names" Timo told the students. At this point, everyone was curious to learn something about Timo's personal life. I actually have two groups of names he said to them. The first group of names is my birth, first and last names which is "Timo Mikwaya." He continued, the second group of names however, is "Kamina To-la-man." Those who select to call me the second group of names are not aware of its meaning indeed. As soon as he finished saying this, few students in the audience shouted, please tell us the meaning of those names so we do not address you with the name that have negative connotations. We would like to address you with "Luzitu" said one of the student because you surely deserve it. Timo was delighted to hear this statement and he thanked the student with all his heart.

Timo continued the explanation, "the first group of names is actually my really name. The second group is my sad nick-names which are related to my height. All the students felt badly to hear this.

After pausing for a while, he sighed, and then he continued "no one sometime would believe that family members can also emphasis wrong nick names on a child, and I am afraid to tell you that the second group of my name was originated from my own mother's mouth. The reason was because she noticed that I was growing very slowly in comparison to many other kids around the blocks. Mama was getting somewhat upset, and for this reason, out of frustration, she would call me *"KAMINA" this* actually means, "Shorty." *ANALEY TO-LA-MAN*, here, Timo sighed prior to giving the meaning, everyone grew very quiet in the room. Then, after a while, he resumed, "analey to la man" this signifies, tiny just like a head of mushroom, laughter.

Students made several comments about this woman remarks. Do you see now what do I mean by the word "LUZITU"or Respect? It is necessary to treat people with *"LUZITU" or respect* regardless of their appearance or their social status. As much as I love my parents, I noticed that my father respected me more than my mother. Probably that is due to the fact that my father came from a modest family whereas my mother came from the royal family.

However, when I was a child I thought my mother really hated me, but looking deep down now, I realized that she loved me in her own way. She just was worried about her son's welfare, because she knew that her son would not be treated with LUZITU in the society due to his small height. I actually understand her point of view now. In general, people are prone to judge prior to analyzing facts. It is always better to find a hidden motive behind any situation prior to making any sort of judgment or drawing any conclusion, Timo highlighted this point.

In fact, my father was my first Teacher, he continued. I learned how to read and write from home. The reason was the following: I know you will find it hilarious in this country, but in my country, they came out with an unacceptable system as far as I am concerned. According to the school regulations, in order for a child to be admitted in the Kindergarten, the child must be measured and should reach a required height, otherwise that child is not eligible to attend school in that particular year. The child will have to wait until the coming year, when it reached the required height.

The school admission is supposed to be dependent upon the child's age, whereas in my country, the system operates differently from yours; it is dependent upon the child's height, laughter!

Therefore I was left behind more than twice because of my height, as you may notice. I really considered myself to be privileged to having a father who is a Teacher. My father taught me really good. When I finally was admitted in School, each year, I was being placed in an advanced class; because everyone of my teacher was realizing that I already knew the material that other kids were being taught. It was below my level. My father, God loves him, so do I; he is really the one who had given me the courage to pursue my higher education regardless to my height. He had repeatedly said, it is God alone who gives the gift. An individual must acknowledge it. Actually, it is so, in order for it to be manifested. Students became so fascinating to hear Timo stories. They had always been eager in listening to Timo's talk. They would wish him to continue talking more about his experience in general while he had been in the Congo.

students rejoiced exceedingly listening to Timo sharing his personal experience of his childhood from his native country. They thought his experience was captivating and very informative.

Students consulted each other, and they realized that Timo was a great help to them. Therefore, they decided to start paying him for his time. Well, he replied to them, I actually thank you very much for your generosity however, if you wish, you can always give the money to the Dean of my faculty, because I am here on scholarship, and I prefer not to get involved into selling and buying transactions, laughter! Students were all surprised to hear this new and strange African Philosophy. He would rather offer us his knowledge freely. Some of them thought he was lacking of wisdom to take that sort of approach.

KAMINA EXPERIENCED A NEGATIVE SITUATION IN BRUSSELS

When he was studying abroad, his grandparents and granduncle missed him terribly. They always kept asking about him and his school progress.

While he was in Belgium Timo used to write to his family and asked about his grandparents and granduncle all the time. He used to assured his family that everything was going just fine. However, he missed his favorite dishes "ntere and mbisi (pumpkin seed and fish) and ntere and mikoso (Pumpkin seed and shrimps and baby shrimps). Timo's parents decided that they would do everything they could to start shipping at least ten baked "*ntere and mikoso*" and "*ntere na mbisi rolls*." They figured five pieces of each will be sufficient to start with.

His parents were instructed to get in touch with airplane Pilot, a family' friend to hand deliver Timo's package, and it was done. Timo was excited and so grateful to the pilot and especially to his parents. He could not believe how easy it was to receive a fresh package from home in a timely manner without any problem. Timo was the happiest lad at the University Campus that day. During that time he did not want to eat anything else, but his favorite dishes from Africa. Three months later, he requested some more, and his parents were so delighted to notice that the first package had reached Timo's hands without any delay or trouble.

Therefore, they decided to ship a double portion the second time. Unfortunately, Timo was not lucky enough this time. When the package had arrived, it was ceased at the Custom Duty at the airport in Brussels. After seizing it, the package was open in order to check the content. When the inspector realized that it was food coming from Africa. The inspector ordered the package to be discarded.

Therefore, the friend brought nothing but the correspondence from his folks. Timo asked the friend anxiously, but where is the package? The friend knew that this was not an exciting news, he hesitated a while to say it, and finally, he sighed. Again, Timo asked the friend I see the correspondence, but where is my package? He asked him. Timo, the friend replied, I am sorry your package has been discarded by the Custom Duty Inspector. He said that he is not going to allow food coming from Africa to enter in the Belgium territory.

As soon as the friend completed his sentence, Timo began shaking with anger. He said, I was looking forward to eating food from home. The food is organic and fresh! And in addition,there is no chemical or anything harmful in it.

I wonder why they have to throw it away. As soon as he completed this sentence Timo began crying really hard. Suddenly Timo lost consciousness fell on the floor. The Dean was made aware, people ran to assist Timo by the time the Dean and other faculty members had arrived, Timo was already helped.

He found on was sitting on the chair, but was still heartbroken. He continued to cry for such unfairness. Many people could not believe to view Timo who was known as a courageous guy crying over his food from home. This is disrespectful and abusive to me, he added still crying.

The Dean called him in the office to calm him down, but Timo continued crying, and added to the Dean I cannot possibly see the reason why they threw away my food. The food is organic, natural, there is actually nothing harmful in it. No chemical or additive in it. This is a special dish; it gives me natural protein. It helps my entire being, and also it contributes in my concentration. Further, *ntere dishes* strength and relax my muscle. Please bear in mind it is because of this food that I was able to grow from one foot to two feet and half now. This is my special diet. I am confident it will help me grow taller than it had been predicted.

After hearing Timo's explanation about this food, the Dean and two other faculty members decided to take Kamina to the airport and speak with the Customer Duty Director in order to request a special privilege if possible. When they had arrived to the airport, the Director noticed Timo's small height, he mumbled, oh, a color

midget, what he wants, he asked his colleague. The Dean and his colleagues said, this gentleman, Timo has some issues to address to you. The Director looked at Timo and said, "What seems to be your problem?" He asked in such a sarcastic tone of voice. Timo ego was eventually hurt, because he was already frustrated, he lost his temper. He said, you know quite well that that food you discarded is organic, and that it does not contain any harmful substance in it. Why in the world you have decided to discard it?

Timo spoke with a deep powerful voice, anyone would think that he weighs two hundred pounds and he is probably six feet five like his father Timoli Mikwaya. The Dean right away asked to speak to the Director and his stuff privately. He told them the reason why that food was necessary for Timo.

He stressed on the fact that it was a part of his diet. He also stressed on the fact that Timo is a very bright student, and he is compassionate, because he devotes all his time tutoring his fellow students free of charge. After listening to all these explanation, the Inspector and the Director granted special privilege to Timo. The arrangement was made from that day to deliver Timo's package from his parents directly to the University's address with a special notation on it.

Things went well from that day until he had completed his study. Timo went to thank the Dean in person after having written a thank you letter right after they had returned from the airport. He still decided to thank the Dean in person and apologize for having lost his temper at the airport. He also wrote a letter to the Custom Duty Director for being willing to make such a special arrangement for him to receive his food from Congo.From that time on, the Dean and his faculty as well as the Custom Duty Director and his colleagues became very close friends of Timo. Everyone knew how intelligent that lad was.

Timo was known to be a very bright student during his undergraduate and his graduate studies. He graduated in both programs with honor.

Prior to returning to his native country, his professors advised him to get his Ph. D, once for all, and so he did. As soon as he had completed his studies, he decided to go back to the Congo, and served his country and his fellowmen. Prior to his return, his professors and fellow students as well as the friends from the airport exchange addresses because they wanted to keep in close contact. Every time they came to visit Timo in Congo, they made sure to bring back with them baked intere dishes.

CHAPTER XIV

KAMINA RETURED BACK TO HIS NATIVE COUNTRY

His parents Mr. Timoli and Denoza were overwhelmed when they became aware that Timo had completed his studies abroad, and that he was arriving from Europe the next coming week. On the day of his arrival to Congo, his parents went to meet him in Kinshasa, the City Capital, along with one of the servants. It was such as surprise, at first to Timo's parents, because they could not recognize him right away, he had grown taller than he had been prior to his departure to Belgium.

Timo appeared about four feet and half tall instead of two feet. As soon as he came out of the gate, he smiled and waved at his parents. His father ran towards him and hugged him first. Suddenly, the father shouted, here comes my Prince! I am so glad to see you again. Shortly after that his mother Denoza, came second, hugged him also, she actually greeted him with tears. She uttered, my son, words failed me to express my joy! Timo hugged his mother and told him, Mama I am extremely happy to see you again, well and strong. Then, they drove to their Town.

The entire Town was excited, because Timo was well known due to his height and his intelligence. Throughout the entire region, Kamina was the first small man people came across with. Some people used to travel miles away to come and see the little man called "KAMINA." They could not wait to see him back. His friends from his childhood were so anxious and eager to see him again. They noticed that Timo appeared taller than two feet and half. In fact, he measured almost four feet and half opposed to what Doctor Moto Pamba had predicted. It was quite impressive.

Upon request, Timo was informed that that doctor was still practicing at the same location; although, at that time he was seventy-eight years old; Timo was also told that Doctor Moto Pamba has never stopped asking about him and his school progress in Europe. Because of this, his parents advised him to pay the doctor a visit in a few days.

Upon arrival at his clinic in order to greet him, Doctor Moto Pamba recognized *Timo's parents* right away, but did not have a slightest idea about *Timo*, because he expected Timo to always remain one foot and half tall, a small man whom he had actually predicted to be, and that was based on his medical expertise.

Apparently, little he knew about Divine intervention. When, Mr. Mikwaya, told the Doctor Moto Pamba, "Look at the person you have been inquiring about!" Doctor Moto Pamba inquired with a serious look on his face, who is this gentleman? Timo's parents and Timo himself realized that he was not recognizing Timo, so they busted laughing prior to specifying that it was, the "ONE FOOT AND HALF CHILD whom you had predicted sixteen years ago! The Doctor almost fainted. His eyes were wide open. Suddenly, he held his bold head, prior to greeting Timo eagerly, and shouting, "This is incredible indeed!" I am truly, so A-a-amazed!! Timo, this is really YOU? He added.

The doctor said, "Timo I still recall when your parents first came in my office, they were torn into pieces, when I had told them about your infirmity. Your mother as any passive being began to shade tears about my unfortunate prediction. Well, God forgive me today, I am only a human, what can anyone expect! I certainly should not have made that false claim. I guess the Lord wanted to teach me a lesson that only "Him" alone who can actually predict anything with accuracy!

We human beings are indeed fallible, regardless to our sophisticated scientific theories, experience such as this one is termed a Miracle to the world. I now see tAnd then, after having exchanged few words, they bade the Doctor goodbye.

CHAPITER XV

KAMINA MEETS WITH HIS OLD FRIENDS

Most of his old friends were still around, and eagerly they got together, and came to greet him at his parents' home. It was indeed such a rejoicing occasion. Upon arrival, Timo began to inquire about few other friends that were not among those present. Timo felt sad that he could no longer see the next door friend whom he used to admire, because he was admitted in school, whereas Kamina was being denied school admission, few consecutive years, because of his small height.

He began asking about them, one after the next. Initially he asked about his friend Lokota, and he was told that he actually had moved to Northern part of the Congo. When he inquired about his friend Masamba, he was told that Masamba joined the Army, and that he had been stationed currently in Kindu Base. Then, he had inquired about another friend called Shandaka, the answer to this was, Shandaka did not do well in school. He dropped out and became a taxi driver in the city of Kisangani. However he has been very lucky. Most of his customers and his close associations are gold miners. He had bought a large home site and built himself a huge house. Actually he is doing pretty well he is married and his wife's father is Greek and his mother is from Kasai region.

Timo continued, what happen to Mr. Mabaya Diba, Timo asked? He was told that actually Mabaya Diba had gone to study in Lisbon, Portugal and he married a Portuguese woman. They actually have three children, two boys and one girl. They lived in the city of Lubambashi. His wife and his children adored the city of Lubumbashi. Timo went on asking about every one of his formers friends

Then he asked "what happen to my friend Telema"? Well, Telema received a Scholarship; she is in Russia at the present time; she attending Medical School. However, since she got in Russia, she has been complaining about the cold weather. She said she missed the Congo's Sun very much. She also said that her room does not have enough heat, and that she always has to warm her bed prior to going to sleep with a hot-water bottle, laughter! Timo had experienced a cold weather, and he could relate to the cold weather better than any of his friends who had not yet travelled abroad.

His friends were just curious; they wanted to hear about Timo's experience abroad. He told them that in general things had gone well. He just related his first experience at the University Campus when he had first arrived. The Dean of the School was not sure that I was capable to study with the tall people, I guess; Timo shrugged. Therefore, he did not let me attend class right away. He ordered that I take an entrance exam. I was tested in French literature and in Mathematics. Actually, the dean's decision was that, if I do not score high, I will not be permitted to attend School. I will have to return back to Congo in exchange with another tall and intelligent student.

It was pretty challenging, and a pretty disturbing experience, Timo said. I just had to do the same way my father did when he was attempting to propose to my mother, the Chief's daughter. When things had gotten out of his hands, he just had to surrender to God and pray. I am glad that I have kept a close association with my dear father, how I love him! He had told me all the miseries he went through in order to marry my mother, a half princess. In fact, my father came unfortunately from a modest family. Therefore bridging the gap between two different family backgrounds was not an easy thing. However, my father had a determination to marry his princess, and he did it. Why was it possible? It is because God had allowed it. I can understand the royal blood is such a great symbol to the family, the heirs must always acknowledge it, but it has its advantage and its disadvantage in the society sometimes, Timo concluded.

However, I accepted that challenge to take that test. My only regret at that time was the fact that I did not bring with me any French literature or Mathematics books which could have helped me to make a quick review. I did not however believe that I will be tested on the University subject matter. I had confidence that any test would be based on the High School level.

Therefore, I knew I will definitely do very well, unless they decide to fail me intentionally, because of my height and my skin color.

I had arrived in Brussels on Saturday evening; I rested the whole day on Sunday, however, in the evening of that day, I was informed that tomorrow, on Monday at 10:00 am, I will be tested. I also was informed that the test will cover general subject matters. The School would like to assess your High School level, one of the faculty members advised me. So on Monday at 9:00 a.m. one instructor in charge came knocking at my door, and took me to the office. I had noticed that everyone's eyes were directed at me. I knew inside of myself that my height attracted all those people's attention. All of a sudden, an office secretary stood at the office threshold, and called my last name, Mik – waya. I have never heard anyone pronouncing my name in that manner, so I did not think she was calling me, and I just sat down there without answering the poor lady.

I had realized that when the school forwarded my information to the University, I had no idea that my nick name KAMINA was also written on that form. Then I heard the secretary called the name, "Kamina;" I was amazed to hear that name in

Brussels. Then I answered, oh yes. The secretary asked me how is it that I did not answer when she had called me *MIK – WAYA*. I told her, I am awfully sorry Madam, and I did not think that you were actually calling me.

The secretary immediately, apologized, adding, I probably mispronounced your African name. How do you pronounce it? I told her that my name is pronounced "*MI-KOUAYA*" and not *MIK – WAYA,* laughter! Further she asked me what name you prefer to be called, Kamina or Mikouaya. I explained to the secretary that actually my first name is *TIMO* and my family name is *MIKWAYA*. So, what then about Kamina, she asked me? I replied that "Kamina" actually was my nick name; it was given to me by my mother. I was actually surprised to hear you call me by this name. The secretary said, well it is written next to your name. I found it very charming that's why I selected it. Timo, added, I see, but chose not to explain the origin of that name or the story behind it.

Concerning the test Timo continued, I could not believe how easy it was! The duration of the test was two hours to complete such a long test. It was nothing new because I was so familiar with the Belgian School system in the Congo. However, I completed the test in less than an hour. However, when I was about to return my completed exam, the instructor in charge warned me, "Sir, please remember you have plenty of time to complete your test. If you have finished you may take the time to review your answers prior to returning it." Then I had replied that I did have enough time to review all my answers, thank you sir, for your concern. The instructor smiled and said, "Timo fine but, I am just trying to help you, because I have never seen any student who had ever completed this long test in less than an hour. This will be the first time, and it would make a history of this department if you do pass the exam, he said it sarcastically, then, he shrugged.

Timo continued, I was then asked to go out of the testing area, and have a seat in the waiting area in order to wait for my test results. I had noticed that the chair where I was sitting was slightly too high for my height. My legs could not reach the floor. However, I could hear people saying, "He is well dressed. He has on a very expensive navy blue suit. He appeared as though, he came from a well do to family." I actually was an object of attraction, and everyone has his eyes on me.

Further the people who were nearby started questioning each other, "who is that small color man?" Timo said, I can hear them whispering. Then I could hear in the background another person replying, "He is a student from the Congo, applying an admission. He is here to take an exam that can qualify him to enter in the University campus. Suddenly, I heard another person asking, "Can anyone tell his age?" It was so funny, said Timo, "people were trying to guess, but their answers were all wrong. I knew that I was eighteen years old but they were shy to come forward, and ask me directly that sort of question. Fifteen minutes later, the secretary stood at the office threshold again and called, "Mr. Mikouaya, smiling at me."

I smiled at her back then she said: "did I pronounce your name correctly this time? Timo said, I told the secretary, "oh, you did very well this time, as a matter of fact you had sounded as though you had lived in the Congo." "She said, "No unfortunately, I personally have not yet been in the Congo, but I had an uncle who lived in the Congo for several years. He had worked for the Mining Company in the Eastern part of the Congo. Two of his children are in fact studying at this University. I am pretty sure they will be delighted to meet you.

Then the secretary invited me, saying "please come on in and entered into the Dean's office. He needs to speak with you regarding your exam."Timo said, "Unless they fail me intentionally due to the injustice of this world or because of my small height, otherwise, I had to pass. The exam was much easier than all the exams I have been passing in the Congo." Timo continued, it was quite an experience, as soon as I entered the Dean's office, he actually stood up and then shook my hand enthusiastically, Mr. Mikwaya, he said: "Congratulation!

I and my staff are very pleased with your test results. You actually had excelled our expectation. Besides, you completed the entire exam in less than an hour! Welcome on board. Our University likes to admit only bright students. Students who will maintain a high reputation of our School are always welcome, he concluded. Well, this is actually how I was admitted in the University campus of Brussels. It was because I passed the test, otherwise I would have been sent back to the Congo. Timo told his friends who were listening to him with a very high interest.

Timo said "when I started attending classes, I made sure that all my readings and papers were done on time. I knew from the beginning that I did not have any close friends to assist me. Therefore, I had to remain focused on every subject, until Icomprehended it. As soon as I began scoring higher than my class mates, students started to approach me more and more. From that time, they began to become very friendly and started to carry open discussions. When students became aware of my ability to comprehend the most challenging subjects such as Math, calculus, Statistics, and Accounting, classmates began to approach me secretly in order to request for my assistance in these subjects.At first it was being done on one to one basis, and then finally I started to schedule at least ten students at once so that I can tutor them all together. Timo loved these courses, and he had a pleasure to explain the subjects to his fellow students free of charge.

Finally, Timo continued, many students who were having a hard time in their studies, heard about my tutoring session. Then, they had joined my previous group. Next thing I knew, professors were made aware about my willingness to assist my fellow students. Gradually, I began to become very popular as I had been in Elementary School and in High School here at home. Next thing I noticed, people around me started to flood me with compliments, and especially female students. As soon as Timo mentioned this thing, all his friends got excited, they were cheering and laughing! Unfortunately, my height stood on the way, and the question of dating was out of my mind all together. However, I did have several female buddies afterwards, again, laughter!

And then, the news spread throughout the campus, and finally the professors became aware of it.. Timo was compassionate with his fellow students that he hardly had time for himself. At the same time some faculty members were concerned that people would take advantage of me because I am a color small man. I was being referred to as, *"A little man with a huge Brain!"* He has got a Big Brain for a little man. He is a genius indeed. He really knows this stuff, and can clarify things better than professors in class, said most of the students. Timo said any excellent gift comes from God, and therefore I gave credit to God where it came from. Timo was so humble. He continued, my fellow students thought it would be fair to start paying me a little money for assisting them. They were afraid that the Dean would feel that they were taking advantage of me.. And so, one afternoon, the students asked me, "Timo what would be the minimum amount of money that you will be willing to accept for all your devotion?

I was surprised to hear this offer? I asked them, "In this country you make your fellowman pay for such a service? " They confirmed that it was so. Then I replied that we do not do things that way. In my country, you offer this service for free, because by so doing, your intelligence and understanding expand. In fact, the more you explain the subject to other people, the more your brain will conceive new knowledge. One student in the audience shouted what a weird concept!" I have never heard anything of that sort, free of charge? Surely that would be the day!

Timo I continued, once you start charging them, your intelligence cannot expand, and you will remain limited. I am sure since I have been here, you heard people say different things about me, based on what they see in me. Some believe that I am a gifted and an intelligent person, and I hear other people referred to me as "a little man, with an extensive brain;" whereas to others, I appear as a "little genius," etc. You probably wonder why? Well, the answer is simple because I always give my help free of charge. The only time that I would accept a fee, would be if I am employed. Otherwise, I feel obligated to offer help for a humanitarian reason. By doing this action, I expect those I help to do likewise to those they encounter.

This means you will tutor other students in need as well, and you would get recognition for good deeds. Timo continued, and then, I told them, in fact in my country, we have an adage that says, "Two Hands must cross with each other in order to maintain the flow of energy in both directions." This simply means that *when you receive gifts from others with your right hand, you should always remember to return your own gifts to others with your left hand."* Do not be in a position of just receiving gifts or help without giving back. This would mean nothing, but "***Selfishness***" which is the great enemy of our society. Furthermore, when you offer a gift or a service from your heart, it must be done with what it is referred to in my country, as "**LUZITU or BOTOSI**" this means Respect. A person must not think that just because he is in a position of helping others, he or she must disdain those he or she is actually helping. Having such an attitude is lack of "**LUZITU or BOTOSI**" to your fellowman; I told my colleagues that, Timo concluded.

Further, Timo said, students used to say that I sounded like a real professor while tutoring. They talked about my deep powerful voice repeatedly in comparison with my small height. Concerning my appearance, I was always dressed up in my colorful African suits or in my African demi-dakar sport jacket during the tutoring session. My fellow students had always admired that view very much.

Suddenly, one of his friends interrupted, and asked, "Were your fellow students benefiting from your tutoring service?" Every one of them had seen an improvement in their own grades, and was willing to pay attention to what was being explained in the class room, he replied. All of them were quite honest, they were really pleased. In fact, they themselves confirmed it repeatedly. I was indeed glad about it.

CHAPTER XVI

THE BEGINNING OF KAMINA'S PROFESSIONAL EXPERIENCE

Timo's Parents were so proud of him. His father referred to him sometimes as my "Little Prince" from the Ancient African Kingdom. They truly couldn't wait to share thegood news with their son's grandparents and uncle prince Mokwe of Zama Village about Timo arrival from abroad. In reality, Timo's grandparents, as well as his granduncle used to wonder whether or not they would ever see him again. Their primary concern was the fact that they did not have any slightest idea how the people in Belgium were treating him? Questions were pondering about Timo's life abroad. Eventually, they were imagining how he was being addressed by those who always place themselves too high, such as the kings and the queens of injustice and prejudice.

His wealthy grandparents always stressed on his small height and his skin color. How do people view him there abroad? At least here in our country people know he has some royal blood, and he will be an heir of Chief Mundu and Chief Mokwe of Zama village. People value these facts when they actually talk about Timo.

Whereas abroad, people probably are undermining him, since those people do not know that Timo has a royal blood in his veins. Those had always been Timo's grandparents and uncle concerns. Therefore Timo's parents had sent one of the servants to bring the good news to his grand's Parents, Chief Mundu and Chief Mokwe to their respective villages. Timo has completed a higher education than his father Timoli Mikwaya. Everyone in the villages spoke joyously and respectfully about it.

TIMO RECEIVED A SECOND OFFICIAL POSITION

Timo was appointed as a governor of the Shaba Region, in the Eastern part of the country. His responsibilities were to control all the political issues in this province including all the mining areas throughout the entire province. Based on his evaluation, he assumed all of his responsibilities satisfactorily. The constituents were pleased to have him as the governor of their province. At first however, when Timo's appointment was announced, those who had heard about his small height spread the news.

Some people were skeptical about his ability to assume such a huge responsibility. They did not think he would have the potential of controlling his administration, because people in that area were known to be stiff neck. Therefore Timo being a small man, he would absolutely be taken advantage, so people thought. Further they were afraid that no one would ever listen to him; the administration would therefore be a chaos in few days.

However, it was proven the opposite, although the majority of the people who worked under his direction, stood much taller than Timo, in spite to this fact, he set a strong discipline, everybody help him in the highest regard, because he was very nice but stern in terms of his work. He had made it clear to every department head from the beginning that his main concern was the submission of their reports in a timely manner. So everyone in each department had a new awareness of handling their duties in a timely fashion. Everyone addressed him as His Excellency, Mr. Mikwaya. His chauffeur Kahulo was six feet tall, and was a very humble employee and showed him a lot of respect. He always carried his attaché-case, and any other necessary boxes from his boss's home to the car, and back and forth. Kahulo also would run forward to open the car door, as well as the office door in order to let Mr. Mikwaya enter. Mr.

Mikwaya received more respect in that area than it had been anticipated. His small height did not matter any longer whether to himself or to those of his associations.

TIMO APPOINTED FOR AN OFFICIAL POSITION

Timo, subsequently, received another higher position. He was appointed as a Commission of Higher of Education. And therefore, he had to move from the city of Lubumbashi where he had previously stationed, to Kinshasa city. His work was done meticulously. The first thing he did as soon as he had assumed that new position was to change the school system. The policy of measuring children's heights prior to allowing school's admission was repealed, abolished all together. Children were being admitted to school based on their school age and no longer based on their height. He was well respected regardless to his small height. He treated his employees fairly and with respect regardless of their levels of education, everyone confirmed it. Minister, Timo Mikwaya had actually exemplified his wisdom, his potential and new knowledge in his performance. He was well known throughout the country. The eminent critics who had in fact believed that being a small man like Timo would be a barrier to succeed in the society had proven themselves wrong.

Timo was no longer looked down but up. Denoza his mother remembered how mean she had treated Timo, calling him name, Kamina (Shorty), and showing him a tape measure, a thing that scared Timo the most, because he knew that after measurements will come that nasty song "Kamina-Kamina".

Further, after the Kamina song would follow the nasty and unkind remarks addressed to a poor child. Well, his mother, Denoza was confronted with the facts of life. Things do not always remain at the status quo. Denoza never thought Timo Mikwaya (Kamina) could be given a chance to hold any positions of trust, which would require workers to show him Luzitu-respect in the society. She had thought her son's small height was a big mountain that stood on his way which no one could ever dare to move. Unfortunately, his small height was melted to nothingness. He overcame the obstacles. His brain gave him a high positions and a lot of respect both in the society, as well as in his own family.

Timo held higher positions than the rest of the children who were six feet tall. When Timo's mother knelt on her knees in order to apologize, Timo quickly ran towards her mother. He said to her, "No, Mama, please get up, he hugging her. He gave her his small hand, but full of potential in order to lift her up. Mama, he said, I love you very much. We both went through an agony with the experience of life. I know you love me as dearly as Papa does. It is understandable, that you just needed to view your son successful in life, and that was actually the vital point.

Certainly Mama, now I understand pretty well all your concerns. You were just worried about the injustice of this world, as well as your royal blood's reputation. Further, you knew that human's pride wants always to show off the best side in order to prevent being mocked at. Truly, it wants rather to gain respect through every necessary means. We have to understand, however that God is the only Creator of everyone and everything, and a human being is not!. Human intelligence is somewhat limited to a certain degree, whereas God's wisdom is just incomparable. The height of a man alone without intelligence in it cannot accomplish much. The intelligence, however, will operate whether it is found in a tall person or in a small man's body. The brain will function!

CHAPTER XVII

KAMINA'S MOTHER'S CONFESSION AND CONFIRMATION OF A GIFTED CHILD

Timo sensed deep down that his mother had a guilty consciousness for her cruel behavior of the past. He wanted to help her get rid of anything negative that was embedded in her mind. It so happened that her mother on her own volition, had approached him, saying, Timo, my son, God is indeed good! Timo gave his mother his full attention hearing this introduction. Suddenly, Timo noticed his mother kneeling down, and then began to crawl towards him, with tears streaming from her cheeks. Timo spontaneously ran towards her Mama, what is the matter, he asked her. Son, she replied, crying, I must apologize for my ignorance of the past, she said. Timo helped her stand up. Mama I am ready, let us seat, and then talk, he whispered. Mama, instead of crying for the mistakes of the past, you should be rejoicing to reap the joy of having a gifted child, isn't so? Timo asked her.

Yes, he continued I acknowledge Mama, that the past had actually brought us some negative experience. I recalled how much I hated to see that tape measure around your neck.

Although, you sometimes had no intention of measuring my height, but was just taking your customers' measurements in order to make their dresses; Mama, it was just a psychological effect, just looking at that tape measure, stirred fear in my mind!

That view made me think that you were about to proceed as you had always done; such as, ordering me to climb on the stool, so that you could measure my height in order to see whether or not any increment has been added to my height. I used to be so frantic, and that was why I used to cry prior to your reaching me. Yes, mama, I would admit, it did disturb me that tape measure at that time. That was the reason why I began refusing to eat at Papa's absence. Timo's mother had sat there, listening quietly. In addition, she was shaking her head, as though to say, how in the world, I could ever act in such harsh manner to my own son? Son, I was just inexperienced mother then, indeed! She added.

Timo continued smiling, you know, the song "**KAMINA**", *KAMINA, ANALEY TO-LA-MANN* used to cut my appetite. Remember Mama, when you used to call me **Kamina** every time you saw no change in my height?

Mama, remember also the day that I jumped away from the stool when you had attempted to smack me with the tape measure, just because you noticed no change to my height? Laughter! Denoza said, yes, I do remember, after I have caught you, you began pleading, *Mama please do not hit me,* Timo laughed so hard here!

Denoza then asked him, do you remember, my answer to your appeal? Timo replied, giggling, yes, mama, you actually had answered me as follow, "Timo the reason I should hit you is, because you had me run after you. You have been disobedient when I had asked you to come back on the stool. Denoza and her son both began really laughing their heads off!

Timo finally told his mother, see mama, you should not continue to condemn yourself for the past mistakes. Now I understand all your concerns, at that time those words sounded abusive. Currently, however, they all sound amusing. Obviously, without those words that brought pain to both of us I don't think I would have been willing to work so hard in school and become a successful man in this country. Timo's mother had found a relief of her pain by crying while her son was bringing forth all these embedded awful things.

Timo also added, Mama your past concern was actually justified. You knew that the world is full of injustice. Certainly, your only consolation regarding my future life had been the heritage which my grandparents and granduncle in the villages had planned to leave me in case of their passing away.

You notice, papa came from a modest family, but he has always been so faithful to his God. It was never a joke when he had always stressed on his slogan, "If God can part the ocean, and God can bridge the gap as well." See, now marriage between modest and royal families is no longer a big issue, Timo concluded.

Timo's mother nodded her head slowly, and added, "son, my faith in God has been growing daily since I married your father, and because of these experiences, with myself, with your achievement and even with your height, the doctor has been proven wrong. Look at your height currently you are almost four times taller than one foot and half which that wrong doctor had predicted. The Power of God is actually "Real," and no joke, son, Denoza concluded. It is awesome

Timo said, "I truly would say that my height today has been my blessing Mama, in spites of everything that had occurred. If I had been six feet tall, I guess I should not have accomplished what I have done today. Hearing Timo's statement, his mother stood up suddenly hugged him; she was emotionally touched. Tears began dripping of her eyes.

Denoza said, "I love you Timo, my prince, you actually had honored me. I was wrong in feeling that our ancestors had punished me for marrying outside of the royal blood. I now agree with your father, who had always believed that it was God's will. I would not let anyone call you" *KAMINA*" any more, but Timo Mikwaya, Luzitu.his will remain your real name. You now deserve all the high attributes, said his mother.

DENOZA CONFIRMED TIMO WAS THAT GIFTED CHILD

His mother said I must give glory to God for having provided me with a real husband who had given me a special and a gifted child whom I had taught he was going to be nothing in this world. His father Mr. Timoli Mikwaya, had faith on his son Timo, although, he was a small man he trusted that God made him a special, and a gifted child. Timoli and Denoza had three children all together.

However, Timo Mikwaya (Kamina) was more successful than the rest of the children. Timo Mikwaya had one young brother. He was as tall as his father six feet and two; he was called Musasa Mikwaya. He was a carpenter. Timo also had one sister called Mami Mikwaya. She was five feet eight tall. She was married as soon as she graduated from High School; her husband was a head Nurse.

CHAPTER XVIII

OFFICIAL TIMO MIKWAYA VISITS GRAND PARENTS IN THE VILLAGE

Timo Mikwaya was being received as a hero whenever he visited his grandparents in their respective villages. His visits were being announced a month prior to his arrival. In order to greet the people, he would climb on the stage built especially for that occasion in order to allow him to deliver a short speech and thank the people for their support, love and their loyalty to their Chiefs, his grandparents. People would make serious preparation to welcome him. Timo would bring and offer them the basic necessity such as: Milk, sugar, Tea, Coffee, Salt, and Soaps. Shortly after delivering his brief speech the Mpuita musicians would start playing and the people would start singing in the honor of Minister Timo Mikwaya.

Timo was considered to be an unusual human being. His height, his education abroad, and his career made him so special. Although Timo had a royal background and had acquired a very higher education, he was humble.

Those who worked for him testified that he treated them with love and respect. Timo Mikwaya was viewed as a very important figure in the entire area where he lived. He was no longer called "Kamina or Shorty" but rather he was being addressed as Mr. Timo Mikwaya, Luzitu (Timo Mikwaya, Respect), Honorable Timo Mikwaya or His Excellent Timo Mikwaya.

There was a song dedicated to Mr. Timo Mikwaya, thereafter. Right after his short speech in the village – The Mpuita musicians would start playing and the people would begin singing and dancing along in his honor.

The following are the lyrics of the song of praise.

Tika kubenga ye Lisusu 'Kamina" kasi benga ye **-Don't you ever address him as Kamina, rather address him as:-**

Oh, tokobenga yo - ***Oh now we gonna address as you***

Tata Timo Mikwaya na Luzitu - ***Mr. Timo Mikwaya with Respect***

Tokobenga yo Mokonzi - ***We gonna call our Chief***

Oh, tokobenga yo - ***Oh we gonna call you***

Tata Timo Mikwaya na Luzitu" - ***Mr. Timo Mikwaya with Respect***

*Tokobenga yo Honorable - **We gonna call you Honorable***

*Oh, tokobenga yo - **Oh we gonna call you***

*TataTimo Mikwaya na Luzitu - **Timo Mikwaya with Respect***

*Tokobenga yo Son Excellence - **We gonna call you His Excellency***

*Oh, tokobenga yo - **Oh we gonna call you***

*TataTimo Mikwaya na Luzitu - **Mr. Timo Mikwaya with Respect***

*Tokobenga yo Prince na Luzitu! -**We gonna call you Prince with respect!***

Prior to returning to the Capital city, his grandparents would take him around the plantations and would make him visit all the farms, the cattle and pisciculture ponds.   His political career was successful. Timo always made sound and wise decisions. Further Timo knew how to take initiatives and make implementations in a timely manner without fear.

Conclusion

Timo Mikwaya, a small man, four feet tall had exemplified his strength, courage, ability, and the necessary intelligence required in accomplishing everything that a six feet tall man would. His parents' marriage had bridged the gap between high class and modest class individuals through his father's faith in God. Further, as a Minister of Education, he had the power to change the School system thereby eliminating the unnecessary admissions' requirements. Timo believed in his father's slogan, "God has the power to part the ocean and God also has the power to bridge all the gaps."

Therefore, the height of an individual can never prevent that person to achieve his or her fondest dreams. Everyone was given a degree of intelligence or a special gift to perform certain tasks better than others. All the necessary abilities to accomplish anything in this world are originated from one Mighty Source, and that is God the Creator of the universe. God has the power to alter any situation if need be.

FINIS

BEPONA BOOKS

Africa Presents:

- The Congo RDC and Lingala Language (English, and French version , level 1 –First edition) **LINGALA/ENGLSIH/FRENCH/DICTIONARIES**

- The Congo RDC and Kikongo Language (English and French version, level 1 – First edition) **KIKONGO/ENGLISH DICTIONARIES.**

- The Congo RDC and Child Education (First edition)

- The Congo RDC and the Congolese Woman (first edition)

- The Congo RDC et la Femme Congolaise (Première édition)

- The Congo RDC and Congolese Cuisine (First edition)

- The Congo RDC and How Tradition Law works in Modern Society (First edition).

- The Congo RDC and Congolese Comedy/Novels

1. A Mysterious boy called Timo Mikwaya well known as Kamina

2. A Western Professor with an African University Student

3. How Can This African Man live with his In-Laws? -

   FOR OVER 15 YEARS!

4. Experience of Two Young African Ladies in America.

Africa presents the Congo RDC and

Experience of Two Young African Ladies in America

Mr. Aleyi Atondi
How can this man live with his in-laws for over 15 years?

Africa Presents the Congo RDC And
a Western Professor with an African Student

ABOUT BEPONA COLLECTION

Our books are written by American of the African descents, particularly from the Congo RDC (located in Central Africa). In fact, the Congolese society is composed of the Bantu Peoples and the Pygmies. These authors of African descents had been compelled to share the Congolese culture with those individuals who are interested in diversity. Our educational books are factual. They are based on our personal research which was conducted scholarly, and confirmed by oral traditions.

Generally, Bepona Collection's books are apolitical. We concentrate our books on presenting the Congolese culture, which encompasses general social issues. Evidently, our contemporary history is connected to our ancient traditions. And therefore, we cannot omit touching some other topics, although slightly, sometimes-when we write about the Bantu/Congolese culture.

Our novels are practically, narrative non-fiction. The names of the characters including the original settings have been withheld intentionally in order to protect the privacy or identities of the individuals concerned.

All our books are written in such a simple language, terms and style. Our goal is to humbly share our culture and to express ourselves, but not to impress our readers.

Kinshasa, the Capital City

of the Democratic Republic of Congo, Prior to the Civil War